THE UNREGULATED HEART

Four Novellas

by

James Roderick Burns

ISBN: 978-81-19654-26-0

First Edition: 2024
Rs. 200/-

Cyberwit.net
HIG 45 Kaushambi Kunj, Kalindipuram
Allahabad - 211011 (U.P.) India
http://www.cyberwit.net
Tel: +(91) 9415091004
E-mail: info@cyberwit.net

Printed at Repro India Limited.

Also by James Roderick Burns

SHORT STORIES
To Say Nothing of the Dog: Flash Fiction (2023)

HAIKU
Crows at Dusk (2023)
The Worksongs of the Worms (2018)

TANKA
The Salesman's Shoes (2007)

SEDOKA
Greetings from Luna Park (2008)

MIXED SHORT-FORM/PROSE POETRY
Chopped Liver (2022)

TRANSLATION
Paris Bile: Prose Poems by Charles Baudelaire, with Introduction and Notes (2021)

ANTHOLOGIES
A Gathering Darkness: Thirteen Classic English Ghost Stories (2016)
Still Standen: A Celebration of the Poet's Life (2007)
Miracle & Clockwork: The Best of Other Poetry, Series Two (2005)

Acknowledgements

Literary journals willing to consider, let alone accept and publish, stories of ten thousand words and up are hard to find. Special thanks are therefore due to the editor of *Scarlet Leaf Review*, where 'The New New Colossus, or All Aboard!' appeared in summer 2021; and to the editors of *Cut a Long Story*, the short story-focused E-book platform, where 'God Is Over All' was published in spring 2024.

Contents

It bears a resemblance to some of those irregular German tales in which the writers, giving the reins to their fancy, represent personages as swayed and impelled to evil by supernatural influences. But they give spiritual identity to evil impulses, while Mr Bell ... shows them as the natural offspring of the unregulated heart.

Unsigned review of *Wuthering Heights*, *Britannia*, 1848

God Is Over All

Prayer after a storm, or signal escape from danger

Thou, in whom alone we live, and move, and have our being, we desire to offer unto thee humble and hearty thanks for that signal instance of the protecting care which we have been permitted to experience. When human aid availeth not, thou art mighty to save. O may we render unto thee alone the glory and the praise.

May the danger to which we have been exposed, stir us up to greater earnestness in our preparation for eternity. May the deliverance which hath been vouchsafed to us – while it fills our heart with gratitude, and our tongue with praise – establish the more our trust in the living God; and make us the more willing to meet danger again, when the discharge of our duty demands it.

Prayer book held in the Eilean Mor Lighthouse
(Flannan Isles, Outer Hebrides, Scotland)

1
December 7th, 1900

RODERICK MACKENZIE WAS a good man, all agreed: decent, loving to wife and two sons, a hard worker – the best of the local keepers – and a chapel-goer, to boot; but best of all (and truly the only aspect of any consequence to the National Lighthouse Board, which sat and listened, unimaginably distant from Lewis, away down in Edinburgh's New Town, at the far end of two hundred miles of frozen cable) he was an observant man, quick to register the detail of a shaded picture, the tiniest shift in composition, to tell a stricken hare from a badger's scuttle, or signs of distress displayed on a lighthouse twenty miles distant.

He made it a practice, in his normal rounds, to check across to the Eilean Mor tower from Gallan Head. He had a small hut nearby – all the locals knew it, and knew also of his double-barrelled shotgun – so it was no bother to bump the doorlatch once in the morning, before wintry gloom descended with late afternoon, and escort the fine brass telescope to his preferred lookout point.

'D'you want to come along, Rory?' he asked his youngest over the stirabout.

Rory shook his head, sprinkled on more salt. MacKenzie had been trying to interest the boy in the life of a keeper since the summer. He'd enjoyed stalking the woods, once or twice, laying down markers and watching as his father set his traps, but still seemed more interested in his schoolbooks, the wooden ships he carved and painted with the Macaulay boy.

'I'm alright. Though I might ask Davey down the burn, this mornin. We finished the body of the clipper, an it's drying.'

'After school, mind,' said his mother from the sink. She liked a clean table before sitting down with her own cup of tea, and tried always to drum the same virtue of orderliness into her two wild sons.

The boy rolled his eyes.

MacKenzie smiled, nodded at both then disappeared into the early dark.

*

Mid-morning, all appeared well with the lighthouse. The intervening sea was quiet, almost glassy, its long grey-blue surface quilted with unceasing motion but barely spotted by the hump of waves. Gannets wheeled in, down the cliffs, swooping past him as they made whatever sorties nature required, out over the vertiginous edge. He needed but a few seconds, after propping the legs of the telescope in a forked board he kept there, within a slot of rock, to register the lines of the tower and take in its import. The Board paid him a small sum – barely fifteen shillings a month – to keep watch for distress signals from the keepers, not to monitor the sweep of the light in its nightly twelve hour course. But being a careful man, he kept an eye on the light as well as he could; he'd no doubt that following the afternoon's check, free of any distinguishing 'trouble' discs on their protruding poles, it would shine its guiding column out into the ocean that night, as it had done for almost a year, until the morning watch doused its flame, and daylight took over as the mariner's friend.

He removed a small book and jotted down sighting time, absence of signals, and placed a check-mark by the date. So much, then, for the 7th. Following the afternoon check – the same, though with fewer birds wheeling about to compromise his vision – so it proved for a further week. Indeed, a further day beyond that.

*

There had been fog, damp and yellow as a sodden sheep, clinging about the headland for days.

'They don't provide reward enough, you know,' said Morag as he traipsed out early to the hut in oiled jacket and cap. 'For this – well, Roddy, for this level of devotion. Safety, I understand – but still … '

'Ach, woman!' said Roderick, slipping out.

Actually he thought these words only, saying nothing, but waving as she stood in the doorway with cup in hand, gathering her skirts about her. It was duty, merely, and where duty called he aimed to respond as best he could, come what may.

On the headland, the wind tore at his clothing with its usual skeletal fingers, rattling the hut's flimsy door and upending the rock-trapped chock for the telescope, flipping it side-over-side towards the edge. But for one skilful, rapid step in the half-light, it would have gone over. Roderick strode back, kicked away any lingering moss around the cleft, then chocked his instrument more firmly. Even the sod appeared to wish to dance in this wind.

He had not seen the tower light for a week or more, it was true; in him this raised no alarm. Despite her grumbles at his pay, he was, after all, paid solely for sightings of distress calls, visual cries for help or other necessary action in the form of suspended, physical signals – balls and such – from poles dropped to the side of the tower. No such signals had he seen. The light each afternoon, as he packed up before the start of shift, had remained locked in the tower, and the strait shrouded in long-lingering, soupy fog. It must lift soon, for the view gave him the collywobbles, thinking of what lay in slumber – or worse, beginning to wake – beneath its rolling idiot sheen.

He was a good man, and not prone to superstition, but heard tell as a lad of the blue men of these waters. His grandfather imparted the tales with a wink, a quick sparking knock of his pipe against the rail of the range, but nevertheless, they stuck. Storm kelpies, he'd called them, lying blue as saltwater just beneath the waves, the gross lumps of their backs breaking the surface every now and then at the approach of a ship. Hailing from the gloom, or the spray, he said they could flick into being above even the stillest water, to better fox the unwary mariner, and talked in fearsome rhyme which the seaman must finish after its kind, otherwise he must surrender the vessel to the sea – and to who knew what terrors of the deep.

'But why, grandfather?' Roddy'd said.

He smiled, up on the headland, remembering.

'Why what, lad?'

Knock, knock – a scattering of sparks.

'Why would they come to the ships, and – and *want* them?'

'Why wid the fae-folk snatch ye from the garden-end, boy, or a hob come rolling doon the glen? Their ways are not our ways. Stay close, is all I will say, and never call across the water.'

*

Now it had been a week and a day: of the tower, nothing. Of the light – nothing. Even of the fog an imperceptible withdrawal to whence such things came. Roderick stood dumbfounded on the cliff, looking out once more. He called to mind the appointment letter – from 84 George Street, Edinburgh, a suitably august address he had never visited, and had no wish to – detailing those signs, indications and situations for which he was paid to look. None included this flat, moveless silence; this featureless panel of a scene, without motion as though perceived through the wrong side of a painted picture, where even the natural motion afforded by the trickery of an artist had been stripped away, and the whole left plain as the day before creation.

He shook his head, looked again. What he saw across the fog-free span chilled his mind, sending runnels of sweat down between his shoulder blades. If it had been a situation in the woods, an ordinary part of his keeper's duties, he felt sure this numb shock would have left him, the knowledge of what to do come flooding in like water to an opened lock.

But still it stayed: the tower, flat and unadorned against an iron sky. No pole, dropped; no discs secured, this way or that, to signal any problem with the light, which he knew must be communicated to Edinburgh on the instant, telegraph charges be damned. He hunkered down. The telescope – which both his sons handled with reverence, spinning its powerful lens over almost as great a span as the lighthouse beam – was the only point of light. It gleamed, brass winking in what little illumination found its way across the sound. Yet it was silent as to cause.

With heavy heart, he removed the chock, secured it, carried the instrument back to its home. He returned himself, talked things over with his wife, even his sons in their own rough way, but retired to bed no wiser or more certain of his position.

Things moved toward Christmas, beyond – into lightless weeks, numerous days without signal. He banked his meagre cheques, still haunting the clifftop, but could see nothing concrete within his instructions, and forsook the telegraph office for the certainties of wood and stream.

The silence stayed with him for years, when later he discovered what had happened, sapping the joy from his days, the spark from his evenings. But on the following year's assessment they found nothing wrong – with Roderick, at least – and appointed him to a further term as watcher over the water, though they did not improve his compensation.

2

December 26th, 1900

IT HADN'T BEEN the best Christmas Day he'd experienced – those at sea took every title – but Moore was out of sorts, to begin with: uncheered, cold, a little resentful of his station, if truth be told. The preparations for relieving the Eilean Mor tower had taken longer than usual, owing to the holiday – there was evidently some miscommunication with the Board, about what he did not know, and further, weather of the worst sort creeping up around the Seven Hunters, frustrating the usual timetable.

Not that these things were his responsibility; rather, they lodged like flies in the general scratch of holiday service, beginning to itch even while his mind was elsewhere.

'In fine fettle, Joseph?' asked the captain, as they set sail at last.

Moore simply nodded. Even a simple 'Aye' seemed beyond him. Six weeks on a savage rock – its edges sheer and ravaged by wind and tide – with two morose companions, switching about an endless round of tasks and shifts in the brute dark, were unappealing at the best of times, though he strove always to do his duty. The relief system, clearly, was to the greater good of the keeper making his rotation off the island, back to the warm bosom of his family. There were compensations, he supposed – as much tea as he cared to brew and sup, in the dense fug of the kitchen; the time, when a man was once used to the blocks of hours, cut thick as doorsteps from the loaf of the day, to read, or to make entries in his diary, where things were slack; even the barren rigour of the sea, smashing relentlessly at the rocks, the acid spray reaching up and over the cliffs, had their charms, should he wish to appreciate them.

But overall he grumped in his soul, and made no proper reply, so the captain went about his appointed business.

*

Two days before they'd picked him up – the *Hesperus*, its ordinary crew, Captain Harvie and all – from the shore station at Loch Roag, nothing was amiss but the weather. Ordinarily they laid in a great store of items for use in the tower, packed tightly into crates and offloaded at the west landing, thence hauled by crane onto the tramway and scuttled up the rim of the cliff into the storerooms. From prior rotations, Moore knew the cargo was sizeable (it had to cover three men for six weeks, possibly longer if the sea would allow no landings, and in all eventualities, not to mention the needs of a great thirsty light pulsing half the hours God sent across twenty miles of ocean): paraffin, coal, string, means of small repair, porridge oats, rye flour, wheat flour, eggs, milk (fresh for those first few, precious days, dried thereafter), jam, salted meat and haggis, honey if it could be found, and tea – always and forever, tea.

Marooned in the shore station, beside a frigid loch – it looked for all the world like a locked in Christmas – Moore tried to imagine a keeper's life without tea, and simply couldn't. All revolved around the deep black range and fat kettle boiling on the plate, the vast Brown Betty, steeped inside and out, the favoured mug and sprinkle of milk, the heaping spoonfuls of sugar.

Tea woke you, when your shift-mate's hand dropped a white-tin mug into your bleary vision. Tea sustained you through many a shift, stimulating hand and eye to their various jobs, soothing argument, washing away the wind-borne dust of summer, the bitter crackle of ice in winter lungs. He thought on, as the wind howled over towering waves and all work ceased, about the thin line of supplies trickling up the cliff, and concluded that without coal, range and lubrication, equally, there would be no light whatsoever. It ought properly be to be called the National Tea Board, for on such fuel the protective web of saving beams lighting the entire Scottish coast was truly run.

But alas, there would be no departure that day, nor the following, either.

Somewhere behind him, in the mess, the shore-workers – stalled in their usual holiday flow – made merry with something stronger than tea. Moore put in his appearance, as much for form's sake as company, then bowed and took himself off to bed.

Outside, the weather lashed on in a most un-yulelike fervour.

*

Two days late, though short of nothing but good cheer, the *Hesperus* set sail at last for the Seven Hunters. Perhaps the season should have made no difference. He did think so, though stopped shy of voicing such an opinion to the crew. Not a man – no, nor Captain Harvie, either – looked even slightly better than miserable on deck, the heavy swell discharging its favours equally to those with their sea legs and others (such as Moore) accustomed more to watching the churn, the deep bellying troughs and fantastical high spindrift, from above, than staring such phenomena straight in the eye. If truth were told, he would rather be off the ship already and hauling trucks along a tramway to the storehouse. A keeper's lot was no fairytale – a damned portion indeed of very hard, very repetitious work, was everything it was – but the station offered a solid root of several hundred feet of rock, cliff and grass, standing high above such tumult.

Once they made landing, that was!

He looked in hope over the billows towards their destination. The mate and second-mate made their way about, seemingly unseeing – uncaring, more likely, thought Moore – with the usual sailor's disregard for the yawning sea. He was not sick himself, or at least not in body; but to his mind there reared in these fearsome swells a threat unmatched by anything on the cliff-top. Even the curious bore-hole, a notable feature of the island, seemingly incorporated into the yard of the tower by nature for observation purposes, did not terrify him – it was inordinately useful in harsher spells of weather to gauge the roughness and reach of the sea by the degree to which, precisely in tens of feet and inches, the crashing tide spouted through the aperture, to then spray about the yard.

There, it seemed, some unseen hand had shaped the sea to a tool.

But here, he gripped the rail as if to stare his way by force of eye alone through the swells. It would not make for an easy landing, he knew, and so it proved: as Eilean Mor came into view, the *Hesperus* rounded the far side of the bay (such as it was) that gave onto the west landing, he felt his mind whipsawing with alarm, as anchor was finally set and he climbed aboard an exploratory first boat for a try at the land. The mates stowed supplies mechanically, seemingly fashioned from the same steel as the winch which would haul the goods up the twisting, malign angles of the cliff.

Already, on approach, something seemed amiss: no flag flew from the tower, the ordinary signal from a crew awaiting – indeed, at this point in the six week cycle, highly anticipating – the arrival of relief, and all the goods it entailed. To counteract this peculiarity, the captain tooted the steam horn as they approached. Nothing was brought forth from the tower in response; no keeper appeared, nor signal from such that the ordinary processes of relief were underway. After a mumbled discussion amongst the ship-mates, to which Moore was not privy, and clearly in some consternation at such grievous departure from protocol, the second mate unhoused the ship's rocket and fired that harsh projectile up the face of the cliffs, where it burst against black-metal skies in a gout of garish flame.

More silence resulted, or as much of that precious commodity – quite peculiar to the senses, at the present time – as could obtain in a difficult, rollicking sea.

No matter. Moore, as representative of the Board, and keeper rather than seaman, must to the fore; so said the voice of duty in his mind, and a small (if quailing) part of him applauded its staunch rise to the call.

But as the boat rocked and sidled, dropped back, feinted, moved every which way but smoothly alongside the landing, his hands and brow spoke a different tale. The mate's oars were sure, masterly, but Moore swore oaths aplenty at the riding swells. Finally they hooked into a spot of calm sufficient to land. The keeper hauled out, relieved as any arctic walrus at the touch of land, and gasped for a moment on the higgledy planking of the landing. After a spell, adjusting his oilskins in the frigid air, he waved the mate back, till he should reappear anon with explanations of this curious, cold and unpleasant circumstance.

*

After a treacherous climb, Moore sat down on the small hillock which marked the end of the cliff-stairs, the top-crane's massive arc. He looked about – back down at the boat, which had rejoined the *Hesperus*; right, along the unforgiving cliffs; left, the tramway, its thin gauge trundling up the remainder of the cliff into the stores beside the tower. Apart from a sharp breeze, carrying the breath of winter, a few stray spicules of ice, all was still and ordinary, if this extraordinary island could ever be so described.

Gathering himself, he stood and followed the tramway up to the lighthouse.

At the entrance gate, he saw no-one, and had to open the gate himself. Whenever he had been on relief in the past, this gate stood open, as though the occupants – and possibly the tower itself, crammed as it was with three cranky personages whose edges began to grate during six weeks inside – were desirous of new things, fresh blood pumping in through the passage.

He proceeded inside, and found again a door, ordinarily open to him, now shut. The kitchen and way to the stores lay quiet and undisclosed behind its stout, cross-braced planking. As he cracked the knob, pushed the door inward, nothing struck him but silence. No smells, perhaps of a meal just cooked and eaten, the workings thereof promptly disposed, as keeper's protocol demanded. There was a slight dry, musty whiff, but this disappeared on the fresh inlet of air as he stepped across the threshold.

Moore looked from one side of the kitchen to the other, from far end to near. All was neat, as he would have expected, yet the very neatness bespoke an odd sort of stillness. He walked across to the range, laid one hand gingerly against the side – cold. He touched the plate, fully now, fingers starfished over the black disc, the pit of his stomach sinking in the sure knowledge no heat would touch his fingers, nor harm come to him from an action so reckless. The plate was cold. He strode over to the hearth, heart beating hard, straining as if to lodge in his throat. The ashes were old, moulded to the shape of their last fall into the grate. He took the poker, rattled it through, and dusty clinker dropped into the pan. It had not been lit for a while, he thought, bending to touch; days.

A great spasm passed through him, shaking his chest and reaching like a manacle around his limbs. His neck bristled as if thrust into a sharp breeze. No one – not the hardiest of keepers, the most stolid man of mainland, or island – could go for days in midwinter without fire.

What in God's name had occurred here?

What was happening still?

He was tempted to take a seat, brace forehead between hands and think out all the possibilities, or saving that, run like a midwife's handmaid back along the cliff to fetch what help could be had.

Calm yourself, man!

Moore was grateful at last for the voice of duty. He pressed both palms to his temples for a moment, bit down into the panic, and calmed himself indeed. He was not a man of tempers, passions; if anything, other men remarked in him a certain phlegmatic dullness of constitution which suited the practice of lighthousekeepering quite admirably. He had ever thought it so, and did not wish to depart from so secure a mooring in his own mind – at least, not till his maker wished to prise him free. He prayed today was not that day. He must buckle down and investigate this mystery.

So steeled, he rose and made his way about the whole of the place: bedrooms (quite normal, the beds made up about as much as he would expect from the keepers, though doubtless not shipshape to a mariner's eye); corridors, unstrewn; stores quite ordinary. He poked through the rations in the top and middle cupboards – about the usual amount of wheat flour, lard and eggs missing, a few straggling bits and pieces left over which he fancied they might have been saving to illuminate the dark ends of the watch: half a cone of demerara, a handful or two of candied fruit. He noticed that the bag of rye flour – oddly, for most would take bread from anything but – was practically empty. Yet what of it? These things told no tales. As for the tower, the paraffin reserves were at their expected level – so too the grease tubs, balls of string, chains and poles for the signals as well as the large round black discs themselves, unshipped from their crate, and unused.

The tower, the light itself gave up no intelligence.

Moore returned to the kitchen, all the flame he had missed in the hearth and range burning now in his mind, which felt frantic, almost hingeless with perturbation. At the scarred deal table he sat, asked aloud of the echoing, wind-tight and empty building:

'What in the Lord's name happened?'

Ducat, Marshall and MacArthur – Principal Keeper, Assistant Keeper and Occasional Keeper, stout men all; he knew them – Ducat, Marshall and MacArthur seemed, though he could not possibly credit it, to have disappeared completely into the briny silence. Vanished. Spirited away, on some rogue cloud or the topmost spike of a vast passing rogue wave, unseen in the charts, unsensed in any sailor's deepest trough of sleep.

There was, he realised, one tale which might yet yield its secrets: the logbook.

He fetched a sigh, and rose again, shivering.

Beside the range was a small, sturdy door, giving on a tall cupboard – not unlike the press in which his mother kept her few trinkets and ornaments, dusted every Tuesday without fail – but this not fronted in glass. Instead it had five solid shelves, holding the first year's logs and assorted other records. Pulling the door completely open, to allow for ingress of daylight, he noticed a thin scrim of dust on the edges of the shelves; such evidence of neglect, even of days' duration, further grated on his nerves.

Quaking, looking about him – though nothing moved in the bright kitchen, a silent, cold and empty nothingness having settled in – he bent to his knees to retrieve the current log, scraping it out from the stomach-high shelf, where once completed it would be promoted upwards by a shelf each time, until the tower had been sending out its light, and keeping its secrets, long enough to shuffle the complete records onto a ship bound for Edinburgh. The dust scraped against the underside. He lifted out the black volume, flipped it over. There was a line of crumbs, toast perhaps, adhering to the back. He flicked them away with a hesitant finger, then hefted the ledger out and into the kitchen's light.

He did not know whether logs were legal records – certainly each tiny, tabulated grain of information recorded about the workings of the light was written, bound and transported to the Board, in monthly bundles – but were it ever so, and he being not a Principal Keeper (so long yet! his mind chimed in) he must violate all protocols and check what news of disaster lay here in the record. Moore drew in a sharp breath, opened the cover.

The heavy stock turned, as it did every day under the hand of the Principal. Back through December, November, October, with weather lessening in force as his eyes skipped the pages; easing into autumn, late summer, then the high days of August and July, when light spilled perpetually over the crags, till beyond midnight, the lamp waiting its turn.

He flipped forwards again. As winter began to howl from the entries, Moore slowed; he hit December and the lines compressed, details forced into the narrow space like mince into a pie in the sixth week of rotation; came to the first week, the second week of the month, and here he stopped.

There were so many entries – against routine, and against weather so severe the keepers had watched the spray and the wind compete with darkness for their attention. Here was an entry for the week before he would have arrived, had their programme of normal keeper (and supply) relief been adhered to. It was in the close hand of Thomas Marshall, if he was not mistaken. His heart took another dive as he recognised his colleague's penmanship, so close and real. Though any keeper could note conditions, occurrences or any other happenings pertinent to the life of the tower on the long slate in the kitchen – a nubble of chalk hung on its own slim chain for this express purpose – formal transcription of all that had happened in the log itself must take place only in the Principal Keeper's hand.

Ducat's cramped, angry notations appeared nowhere in the week. December 12th, Marshall's entry began,

Gale, north by north-west. Sea lashed to fury.

This caught Moore's attention – not so much its phrasing (though in his soul he cursed Marshall for an old woman, or worse, a poet) but the nature of the information it conveyed. It was not uncommon for such storms to blow up and rage for days, or a week, even, taking the missing three men somehow through to today's eerie calm in its violent path.

Stormbound. 9 p.m., the entry continued. Never seen such a storm. Everything shipshape. Ducat irritable. (This too, tallied, with Moore's experience.) 12 p.m. Storm still raging. Wind steady. Stormbound. Cannot go out. Ship passed sounding foghorn. Could see lights of cabins. Ducat quiet. Macarthur crying.

Moore paused, finger beneath this last notation. It seemed extraordinary – a stolid lighthouse keeper, and one of Macarthur's length of service, too – undone by a mere storm! All around him the silence spoke, whispering of strange things, and stranger suppositions. What might drive them to such outlandish entries, and in an official log, beyond the commonplace of a storm, on a windy crag in the face of the wild Atlantic?

He read on.

December 13th. Storm continued through the night. Wind shifted west by north. Ducat quiet. Macarthur praying.

(This, Moore surmised, was more in keeping with the man's nature. Crying did not befit a keeper, but a certain measure of faith – indeed a great cargo of it – did not go amiss in the lonely arms of the sea.)

12 noon. Grey daylight. Me, Ducat and Macarthur prayed.

Then, for no reason he could fathom, came a gap in the log of one whole day. Nothing was recorded for December 14th; no space, or torn corner, no tea-stained portion blotted down or overwritten, or simply torn free for whatever reason. Simply nothing. The white space was given over to the following day, as though 15 followed 13 in every diary in the world.

As he read the short (and hopeful?) note, Moore's veins seized as though some crazed hatter had broken in and squirted them full of mercury.

December 15th, 1 p.m., it read. Storm ended. Sea calm. God is over all.

Nothing else was there in the ledger – he flipped about with shaking hand, back and forth, hither and yon, hoping against hope – but nowhere in any ledger, log, record or other mark of passing time recorded in any lighthouse in the world could such an entry occur. Moore sat back, astonished. A runnel of sweat descended, was wicked away into his undershirt like the pass of a child's hand through a winter stream.

He closed the log.

Moore shook, and feeling unmanned, seized one shivering hand in the other, then stood and paced the storage room, fingers clamping and releasing with the compulsive quality of a gate loose in a storm.

Eventually, he realised, he must act – beyond simply reacting. He tore away a strip of linen from his kerchief, doubled its ends and marked the days of interest – such terrible interest! – then slid the log into the canvas pouch used to carry material down to Edinburgh. He placed it under one arm and retraced his steps through the cold, silent rooms, noting their stasis as he went: beds ruffled, but neat enough; doors ajar; range and hearth dark with days-old ash.

Outside, the blow-hole's mouth threw forth a few feet of water, and watching its spume borne away on the breeze, he pulled the outer doors to, locked them tight. Under his arm was a weight of canvas, but heavier yet, of sickening worry. Down the tramline, out to the top of the cliff, he reached the western landing where the *Hesperus* bobbed safely out a hundred yards, or more. He waved, shook the canvas parcel up above his head as though its dull mealy square could summon all the help of the Board, or powers yet undisclosed, which could mystically penetrate this darkness, set all disorder immediately to rights.

As the men in their small boat set out once again for shore, he dropped his arms and stood waiting, numb in the afternoon cold.

3

December 15th, 1900

LIFE AS A keeper – within the tower, in the lighthouse and surroundings – was a little like a dance, it seemed to him. He had not long experience, having been appointed as an Occasional Keeper less than a year before, and serving after only a month's training at the pleasure of the Board, but a year or so was enough to form some initial impressions in Donald Macarthur. The dance was slow, treacly, even; had three partners; moved in planes and small platelets of time, inside larger four-hour blocks, like the crazed dance marathons he had heard of taking place over several days in the United States; and, most worrying of all, involved no choice whatsoever in the matter of one's dance partner.

He hadn't expected perfection, and did not get it.

Ducat, the lengthiest in service and seniority, had experience and wisdom, having been a keeper for more than twenty years, and a Principal Lighthouse Keeper for almost five; Thomas Marshall, as Assistant Keeper, had worked in the job for five years, also, and had periods upon the sea before that, though he remained under thirty years of age, all told. Both men on the dance card were therefore, in Macarthur's view, solid and dependable, as far as their professional experience went. He could not doubt them; did not.

When the *Hesperus* departed, six weeks before, missing one man who ought to have been there but had fallen ill, and thus including Macarthur in his stead, he had no complaints. He might learn a little in this deployment, from a principal and assistant with so much knowledge to share. Yet, as the dance progressed, and days of first acquaintance turned slowly into weeks of familiarity, he admitted to himself that such bountiful dreams of learning must be put aside, for the hard-bitten, gritty day-to-day reality of the tower, and its own painful lessons.

The crane affair, the letter from Edinburgh, had not helped – that was most assuredly so. It came first to his mind on waking, no matter the shift, and talked with a thin and ghostly voice – like the memory of a hard wife long gone, echoing down the corridors of the day – and would not let him rest.

Even now, folding dense, risen rye dough into his own breadpan (the others stuck to wheat, and he was happy to oblige them) it seemed the matter must continue to have sway, whatever rest he craved.

*

It had been his fifth or sixth week in service, eight months before; he didn't properly recall. He hadn't yet entered the tower proper, was merely substituting for a sick colleague; had barely begun the cycle of training and movement in and out, at the Board's pleasure, as an occasional keeper, learning the trade while filling holes as they arose around the vast coast of Scotland. But Marshall was here, alright, at that time; on Eilean Mor. He made that abundantly clear.

Over breakfast, when Ducat had limped off to bed – bashed his leg on the winder, he said, but Marshall suspected one of his moods – he cornered Macarthur at the range.

'What's that you're frying there, Donald?' he asked.

Macarthur looked around, taken aback. When each man rotated onto weekly cook's duty, whether he liked it or not, whether or not he was particularly skilled at the job, there came with the position a certain space and consideration.

It did not do to assail the cook, and most certainly not at the range.

'Back ye go, Thomas,' he said.

'Sorry, sorry.'

The taller man sat himself back down at the table, gave the Brown Betty a theatrical stir.

'If you must know,' said Macarthur, 'it's a slice or two of rye toasted awhile, then fried off in the fat leftover from your bacon.'

'Oh, aye,' Marshall said. 'Is that to your taste, then?'

'It is. More the texture, perhaps – for rye holds flavours inside its depths, you see.'

He hoped the brief revelation would stand off whatever mood was brewing in his colleague, for all he wanted was tea and silence, after another long night. But the other man had scarcely begun.

'I see – yes, indeed!' This rather brittle formality was followed by a bitter laugh. 'I have a notion far less tasty held inside myself.'

Macarthur flipped his bread once more, held it briefly, dripping, over the pan, then put both slices onto a fresh plate and took it over to the table, where he lifted the Betty himself and poured the first of many cups of tea. It boiled out in a burn-brown stream from the high-lifted spout. They were long out of fresh milk, and he secretly detested the gritty powder, so waiting for a moment for the froth to clear, he added sugar and took it black.

'Have you something you wish to tell me about, Thomas?' he said. Better out than in, in such close confines; though still relatively new to the dance, he was nonetheless adept at reading the face of his partners.

Marshall shifted about on the stout grass weave of the kitchen chair, brushing his moustache with the back of his hand, rearranging his legs beneath the table. When he was ready he brought the handle of his mug so it stood square before him, planted both hands on the warm sides.

'I do, yes, Donald – that I do. Better it is that I get it off my chest while Ducat's away to his bed, than cause any further scene with him around.'

'Is it by chance the letter from the Board that concerns you?'

Marshall looked askance, but for a second only.

'Yes – that's it!'

The words burst from his lips like a wave through the blowhole, and there shone in his eyes the same dazzled light as flashed through the sky on the eve of a storm.

'That is it, indeed!'

'Then have at it, man.'

Macarthur crossed his own legs, took a large slurp of tea and sat back to listen.

*

'Are ye sure you want to hear this, Donald? Well, never mind. I wish to tell it.'

He looked in the direction of Ducat's room. The stout black door lay shut.

'It was – what? Eight, nine months ago, and everything was fine. Not so bad. Calm, anyway. There'd been a bit of trouble beforehand – the crane, you know; sometimes the waves will overtop things, knock down whatever they find. It had happened, I won't deny it. But we'd run about like chickens in that bad weather, and were still standing to tell the tale.

'So Ross – he was third, then – Ross fetches the usual bits and pieces beyond food and what have ye, from the relief boat. And there's the canvas packet – from Edinburgh, ye ken? The packet, only that's the Principal's bailiwick, so I wait till Ducat's good and ready to open it, and see what's what. I made the tea, I think, even.

'So we're all three toward the cusp of the midday shift, sitting round, not awaiting lunch, for it wasn't quite that time, but drinking tea, and he says, Ducat that is says, “I have some bad news, men.” Like that, as though he’s up in the blessed pulpit! My heart sank. He’d been leafing through papers while the tea brewed, but nothing showed on that long thrawn face of his.

‘Anyway, “I’ve bad news,” he says, and we both put down our knitting.

‘“You’ll recall that small trouble with the crane, the replacement after the wave, and so on. The Board has written to me – has written to *us*, through me as Principal – with some words, which I must share with you both.”

‘I’m remembering this as though it was written down inside my head, Donald, but ye’ll no need such recollection for the rest of it.’

He rummaged in his pocket, pulled out a well-worn scrap of paper folded four or five times down hard lines, as though snapped open and then harshly refolded many times. ‘I made sure to get a copy after the reading. So, he stands up, you’ll understand, perhaps for gravitas, and he walks to the window so the sun’s at his back, and he reads.

‘“Sir,

‘He says,

‘“Referring to your letter of 24th February last, reporting the accident to the crane, while under manipulation by Mr Marshall, one of your Assistants, I am to call your attention prominently to the circular which was issued on 18th February, 1898, (of the contents of which both you and Mr Marshall are aware, and of which I enclose a copy), holding you responsible for seeing that the crane, hoisting gear, etc., are kept in a sound and efficient state and are in every respect reliable, etc., etc.”

‘Well hell, man! Yes I was aware; we all were. A man lost his life at Sule Skerry when a crane collapsed! But it didnae mean things were the same at Eilean Mor. It did not. But anyways, says he, reading on,

'"This circular is sufficient to impress on you the absolute necessity of exerting the utmost care and attention in the use of the crane, and it would appear that, on the recent occasion there must have been thoughtlessness, at least on Mr Marshall's part, or the accident would not have happened."

Marshall said nothing; merely glowered, continued.

'"Fortunately no one was hurt, but, as there might have been very serious consequences, I have to impress upon you and the other Keepers at the Station, to whom you will read this letter, not only to bestow such care upon the crane and its machinery and tackle as is necessary to keep it efficient, but also to be very careful in the handling of it. The foregoing remarks also apply to the landing derricks.

'"Your obedient servant, James Murdoch, Secretary."'

There was silence for a moment, and Macarthur thought he knew from where such festering unhappiness came.

'So, Thomas, you are sore because of this reprimand, then? Do you not admit any fault in the matter, as we all must, from time to time?'

'I admit entirely to the charge of carelessness. I had been on my feet all night and half a day without ceasing, through high winds and waves that would peel the skin off your back as soon as lap over your feet. No man could have behaved perfectly, under such conditions.'

Macarthur was puzzled. He stirred the pot, added more sugar and freshened his cup.

'Then what has you sore?'

'Don't you see, man? Ducat might have taken me aside before announcing to Ross, and the whole world for all I know, that the Board had singled me out for my sins! He might have prepared me for the lash, but he didnae. He *did* not do it.'

*

Now, five or six months later – he was sure Marshall could cite the exact date, both of the public reprimand and the point at which he spilled his rage to another colleague, possibly infecting a second man of the three-man crew with long-harboured poison – Macarthur felt far more secure in his skin, a keeper's skin, than he had at the outset. He didn't know how, or why, the change happened eight months back; he knew only that it had occurred.

He could speculate, and might so do when they got through this spell of fierce weather and into the balmy straits of spring. Then he might unravel some other small mysteries. Why did Ducat take so lofty a tone at times, far beyond that of Principal – which all might expect, for as the earlier episode proved, it was his neck upon the Board's block when aught went awry – and almost achieve that of preacher, looking down upon two lesser beings at the foot of his pulpit? What exactly had calmed his fellow keeper, Marshall, in the following six months of work, from rage unburdened tender as an ulcer unlanced, to his present state of almost vegetative calm, plodding through scene after scene of daily drudgery like the settled professional man he had assuredly not formerly been?

Ach – who knew!

Macarthur was back on cook duties, and should cease mithering and bend his mind to breakfast. It had been an uneventful shift. Ten to two, and aside from the usual trips up and down to the lightroom and mechanism, sprung but ever-hungry for tension as it wound down to the base, he had spent much of it in this same kitchen now suffused with morning light. In the darkness – with, to be truthful, the fitful, warm illumination of both lamp and range, pushing back the fingers of the dark – and in the unavoidable, reverberating crashing of wind and wave, he had fought to stay alert, and though he had come off shift and slept a little, was still feeling its effects.

He shook his head, tried once again to reassert the keeper's most valuable asset – stolid endurance, proof perpetual against storm, exhaustion and the shrieking of the Atlantic alike. His colleagues would soon be making their way to the kitchen, and would be most displeased to be greeted with small tea and less breakfast.

Macarthur looked about him, still had a few moments to rectify this slip.

He was breaking apart two thick cuts of black pudding with the edge of a knife when the first of his colleagues arrived. Ducat came up to the range, leaned in, sniffed.

'Smells good, Occasional.'

'Indeed. Are you ready for it? We've still some bacon, I believe, though it's growing leaner, and I'm able to fry a couple of slices of bread.'

The Principal Keeper nodded, unwrapping his scarf; shivered, then nodded more fervently.

'Bread and bacon, all in together, if you please.'

He made himself comfortable at the table, freshening the Betty with a deep stir.

'I shall wait till the Assistant arrives, before embarking on a discussion which concerns us all,' he said.

'Oh, aye? The weather, I'm to assume?'

'That, and other things, chiefly operational.'

There was nothing more forthcoming, bar the slurping of tea, the intermittent howl of the wind, and the wallop of high waves in the blowhole. It was a few minutes before Marshall came in, similarly famished. Macarthur had sliced a white loaf – almost gone, since it came from the oven last night. His own rye lay splendid, barely molested, in the pantry, and as the other man settled in he cut himself a fat slice, toasting it lightly at the grill, before dragging it through dripping.

'Are you coming to table, Donald?' said Ducat.

'Aye. One minute.' He pressed the rye deeper into the fat, and was rewarded with a healthy sizzle. 'Just bide yer time one minute more.'

Then they were seated, all three about the table: tea, meat, bread and fat; sugar; steam and fug. After a quick grace, they talked.

The wind outside scoured the windowpanes as though to get a better hearing, but the room was sealed, impenetrable by design to all possible incomers, and it screamed away over the cliffs in high dudgeon.

*

'So, men,' Ducat said. 'Tis – ' he took a look over his shoulder to the mantel clock, 'almost nine, of a fine morning.' He smiled. Outside, the wind – not still or inactive the bleak night through – now raged as though personally affronted; rain threw itself in spiny handfuls against the glass, on all sides; the run-off streaked away in runnels, and even a foolhardy gull could be heard, lofting above the maelstrom. 'Perhaps not so fine.'

The others gave smiles which might have pared the last grains from a rind of cheese, Marshall's honed, in particular, to a gleaming sharpness.

'We find ourself,' Ducat continued, slurping a mouthful of tea, 'at somewhat of a juncture, you ken.'

Macarthur nodded. The fried rye had made its way into his nether regions, chasing the soft, floral black pudding, and all combined with the damp charge of the brew leant his frame an easy lassitude, almost a pliancy, it rarely enjoyed. A pipe, some silence, and the storm be damned – it could be a perfect morning.

Marshall fidgeted, cutting his eyes left and right, lifting the worn handle of his favourite blue tin mug to his lips, then dropped it back, unfulfilled.

Ducat seemed in need of no audience. Pausing now and again to wet his throat, he continued.

'As you are aware, and as is usually specified in the quarterly memoranda from the Board in Edinburgh, routine, structure and punctilious attention to detail are the watchwords of a keeper. I have no doubts about either of you, on that score. The slate – and the log itself, whose detail I alone can transcribe, and do regularly, as you know – attest, I would say, to the efficient operation of this lighthouse. Now, the weather has been – ah, unusual, I would say, of late. Unusual, yes. But there remain the rest of the morning's tasks to attend to, including seeing to these pots, preparing the next meal, and – Marshall – accompanying me to the tower to see to the frankly unacceptable state of the lens. If you are both agreeable, we can discuss after our meal has been squared away what measures will best serve the interests of the Board in the matter of the weather, and any attendant issues. Are we agreed?'

They all nodded, set about their tasks like the grinders they were: slowly, precisely, attentively, solidly; in short, not allowing of prolonged speculation about the afternoon's debate.

That came soon enough.

*

While the men worked, the weather worsened. It did not do so from spite, or some other inscrutable motivation; the waves did not mount the cliffs, smashing against dock and stair and high crane, for their own savage amusement, but from the unknowable mysteries of creation, the fickle lash of the storm. Like bright lances, they speared through the blow-hole, fountaining eight and ten feet and more, then breaking apart over the icy cobbles. The winds, too, lost no time in mounting ever-higher. Not content with penetrating every fold in the bedclothes, they whipped about tower and storehouse, tramway and retaining wall, looking for an entrance into the warm environs of men; or perhaps blew madly for their own dark reasons, or for none.

The keepers were too busy to pay attention, though all three felt the simmer of the storm, its red hand gloved inside natural splendour.

Only when tea called, and food came to table, did they finish their intended tasks and come together. Macarthur cooked, brewed, and brooded. Marshall simmered like his cup. Only Ducat, in his majestic Principal's place, sat unmoving as the rocks against which mad waves dashed their brains, and waited.

Inside his breast pocket, a finger stroked the earlier circular till its fold ran sharp as a penknife, the blade's pressure peaked, and split the paper.

*

'A fine kettle of soup, Macarthur!'

He looked at Ducat, then Marshall, then down at the plate in front of him. He had toasted a couple more slices of rye, thickly buttered them, then run out of appetite. The butter lay in a nibbled stripe around the side, white and sunk, here and there, in the cracks of the crust.

'It was Scotch Broth, James – no more. You've cooked many a kettle yourself, in your time.'

'Nevertheless, most wholesome, and we thank you. Don't we, Thomas?'

Marshall toyed with his fork, making a brittle rattling on his bread plate, but said nothing. Ducat ploughed on. He hooked his thumbs into the watch pockets of his waistcoat, sat up straight.

'As you will both recall from earlier today, the weather on this fair isle has – of late – proved somewhat unexpected …'

'How so?'

Macarthur scratched his chin and took a look at the window.

'Quite expected, I should say, James. We're facing the Atlantic in midwinter, unshielded by God or man, and whatever's out there can make its way in here whenever it pleases.'

'Alright, Macarthur. I understand. It is expected but greater in intensity than a keeper would normally see. Does that meet your exacting specifications?'

'It does.'

Macarthur looked for a moment longer at the senior officer. Perhaps it was the light, the flickering momentum of wind and wave, but was there a slight bluish cast to the man's face, under its great moustaches? He recalled a friend's tale of some new entertainment, in the great city of Glasgow. A music-hall, stripped of stage and accoutrements, with a great flat canvas stretched across the front and some mad fellow tickling the ivories beneath. A clicking, ticking reel ensued and images were thrown upon the canvas, like a magic lantern, but bigger, and not looped round as in the child's entertainment of old. This was a maiden chased across an open field, a train moving towards the watcher, a dog barking and doing tricks for biscuits from an unseen hand. His friend reported that each figure glowed and flickered in a similar way to this, in the present light, and that the hue on their ghostly faces was the same sort of washed-out, somehow ghastly, blue.

The lamp guttered in a sudden draft, then found the wick again and recovered its light. Macarthur blinked. Marshall was his usual pasty self, and Ducat – who for these few seconds, it seemed, had been content to continue talking without an audience – remained flesh-coloured and quite ordinary.

'Nevertheless,' he said, 'you'll both understand there are duties outside this tower which must be undertaken with the same alacrity, the same diligence, as duties within it, no matter the conditions.'

Ducat paused, looked sidelong at Marshall, who squirmed and picked up the Brown Betty to see if any further warmth lay in its dregs. He sloshed the pot in desultory fashion, did not look up.

Ducat looked from one to the other, ticking items off his fingers.

'There is the general state of the western landing – dock, steps, handrails, and so on and so forth. We know from the – ah, we know from the *incident* February last that aspects of the general approach to the station are vulnerable to aspects of weather unduly strong, or out of the normal pattern.

'There is the tackle box, ropes and what have you. These, though supplemental to the physical furniture of the dock, as it were, are nonetheless important – and clearly regarded as such by Edinburgh.'

Marshall flinched at the same moment as a dark shape flitted past the window, cutting the storm light into bars. Macarthur watched the shadow come and go over the backs of his hands.

'There is also,' Ducat continued, 'the crane, tramway and assorted machinery of haulage and disposition towards the top end of the landing. These, then, are what we are charged with maintaining. These, as Principal, I say we *must* inspect and where necessary, repair. It has been several days of exposure to unusual forces, gentlemen. I fear we must proceed outside.'

Macarthur was about to make some mild remark when Marshal sprang to life.

'I don't see, James, why we must – *must* – do anything. Not at all. We are the keepers, are we not? Not those men in their fancy frock coats and hair-curlers, down yonder in Edinburgh. Why they lie as far from the centre of things as the boat from the bottom of the ocean! They entrust us, they pay us, to know when and how to check upon our things, which while they doubtless belong to the people of Scotland, are in truth *our* belongings, *our* responsibility, while we lie in beds paid for by the task, eat food prepared to nourish our limbs in the pursuit of the task! I say – '

But his next utterance, if he made one at all, was drowned out by the huge blue-black flash of a bolt of lightning. Wave and wind followed, their great resounding boom, and the light in the room altered its shade – not subtly, this time, but all of a piece: the three men's faces dropped into black, came out blue with the snuffed lamp, the long arcing shadows of an afternoon darkened early.

'Hold, men' said Ducat. He stroked his moustache, held up a warning palm as the latest high cracking of the storm rolled over, the rain lashing merciless against the thick panes of glass. When it calmed, or seemed to have done so, at least a little, he resumed.

'The weather, Thomas, makes my case for me. The Board's, too.'

'What do you mean?' Marshall was wide-eyed.

'Simply that such force outside necessitates our investigation, that is all.'

Macarthur said not a word. He sipped his tea, took a renewed interest in the white-flecked crust of rye. It was not appetising, yet there remained – at least in prospect – an afternoon of straining physical effort, and so he broke apart the crust with his fingers, ate it in small unthinking bites.

'But such presence could be – nay, would be! – a danger to our lives, surely!'

'I fear it matters not. We must. That is an end to it.'

'How can – '

Marshall was warming to his theme when a particularly large gust came whining up the cliff, taking off loose, sea-worn flakes of stone, stripping handfuls of sodden grass and bypassing the gouting blow-hole. It slapped finally into the loose crevices of the outer door, which banged open like some demon throwing wide the gates of Hell.

'Never mind, man!' Ducat shouted, though he need not have bothered. All three were on their feet and racing for the doorway and the oilskins, ridged boots, weatherproof caps and the long woollen scarves that, hung for days damp and unused, curled about each other like scorpion tails in some desert-bolthole.

They must to the cliff, and landing, then; must go outside, whatever dangers may come.

As the door closed behind them, bolt resecured, and the lamps shivered in the last breeze, there came a sigh from the range. Macarthur had nudged the kettle onto a plate before they left, a quick unthinking motion, and nudged it back when the gale intruded, springing the men into action.

Now the inch of tepid water, boiled for a minute but bound to cool, gave out its last faint breath of steam.

*

Macarthur gasped. Immediately, the flying rasp of saltwater – borne up and onwards, ever onwards, by the wildest of winds – sucked away his air, left his throat parched as though the gallons of tea they'd drunk that morning had been nought but mist. He flapped for a moment like a landed fish, then drew the crinkling end of his scarf out from the oilskin, arranged it around his face. He was about to shout a warning to the other men, who had outmatched him by a few yards, but realised the gesture was useless. Facing the long walk beside the tramway, they heard nothing but the raging sea.

He leaned in, head tucked as best he could, but still the blades of the oncoming wind – keen with spits of icy spray – razored his exposed cheeks. He saw the leaning bulk of the other two stray towards the edge, pull back, stagger on in the furious gale. They stopped, turned. Ducat signalled with one thick-gloved hand.

'Come on – for the stairs!' he seemed to say, though Macarthur heard little. Not even the most foolhardy of gulls would brave the scoured rockface this afternoon.

Soon enough, the three stood slack-jawed before the top of the landing stairs. Ordinarily, there would be nothing much to arrest the attention – a sprouting of hardy grasses; the end of the tramway, as it abutted the outer reach of the crane; a twin-track of rails, one tacking close to the edge, one to the sheltering wedge of cliff, set fast so that men's hands might be secure even in the foulest weather.

Now it was not a sight any expected to see, at least not in their most sorrowful dreams: where the tight rail had hugged the top edge of the cliff, there was a yawning absence – rails burst asunder, as though flicked by some massive hand, where it found them inconvenient to its path, then crumpled by main force into a twist of papery metal. The grass was bruised, smashed down, sodden; the end of the tramline – fashioned quite deliberately, MacArthur remembered, from high quality steel, built for the ages – was snubbed and bent over backwards. The small sleepers that pinned it to the rock were nowhere to be seen.

Yet startling as this was, it paled beside the crane – or should he say, the crane's remains.

'Lord, Lord,' said Ducat, not blaspheming. His voice was sharp, breathy, but cut through the shrieking wind like a blunt knife hacking at wood. 'Macarthur! Marshall! Away a few feet, see if it lies distraught as it seems!'

Marshall gritted his teeth, pulled the slippery beaded oilskin about mouth and nose, then holding fast to the twisted shreds of handrail, edged a few feet down the top stairs. From ten feet back both other men saw his head shake fast, first in disbelief, Macarthur thought, then in answer to his superior's question.

It was odd. Out here, in the wild elements, away from all that was safe and known, Macarthur expected to feel fear: trepidation, at least, where God alone knew what damage had been wrought, and was yet to be worked by mad fathoms of water and a gale half the length of the Atlantic. He expected nerves, a sour stomach, heart quailing within him, both for self and comrades in these unrelenting furies.

But here he stood – feet inches from eternity – and the strangest, blue-warm roseate peace was stealing steadily into his bones.

'Marshall!' he yelled, seeing at once the other man's footing begin to slip. Macarthur lunged with the grace of a diving seal, secured his man by the top of the arm and yanked him back from the cliff like a fish secure on the line. Ducat nodded, then scowled.

'Marshall, beware! Have a little more caution about you!'

Marshall, for his part, shrank back inside his oilskins, leaning as far as he might into the sheltering, soggy embrace of the torn cliff.

'It's gone,' he said simply.

'What?' said Ducat.

'*Gone!* Beyond repair, man; ruined, away with the faeries. Gone!'

And from their slim band of rock, the crane seemed sorry indeed. What was not torn, was twisted, and what not twisted simply shorn away – storm-tossed, stripped as a broken log barrelled away into the night, useless to all. Macarthur stood with bulging eyes. What power was this, that had wrought such comprehensive – yet effortless – destruction? He could see similar thoughts on the half-covered faces of his comrades, Ducat's twisted into a moue of unhappiness, shading to deep thoughtfulness; Marshall's simple disgust. He leant forward, waved his hands backwards towards the safer drift of the cindered path back to the tower.

'What, man?' said Ducat, when all three reached a point of relative safety.

'You do not think this – well, *this*, warrants discussion, sir?' said Macarthur. The crazed blue light of the storm, far from inhibiting his thoughts, seemed more to have liberated them, releasing his mind into some space of clarity bright and clean as a calm summer sea.

'There is no discussion. I must – '

Thoughts of Edinburgh, responsibility, perhaps career were flitting behind the Principal's bristling moustache, Macarthur knew. But it did not matter. Like blue-paper, a diagram, he saw the next few minutes mapped out in space and in time, as though beneath an architect's lamp: with the February incident fresh in their minds, there could be no question of stopping; one, two or all three must proceed – like some unwitting human wave – over the twisted lintel of the cliff-top, down stairs salted to glass by constant water; and finally to the much-abused dock, first receiver of any strange, blue-black favours bestowed by an enraged sea. There was a curious warmth to the idea; he took it inside him, wrapped keen arms around its glow. He felt, almost, as though his limbs were lit with holy truth.

'I understand, sir,' he said. 'But Edinburgh will not simply intuit what we see here – it must be described, then the paper carefully-considered, blotted and entrusted to canvas, oar and railway as a most precious cargo. We cannot describe, but for having seen. Therefore we must see.'

Ducat stared at him from piercing eyes. He cast a darting look about him, to cliff, black cloud, dogwind and thunder. Each man could picture tall fangs of brine stabbing and smashing at rocks till in desperation they crumbled.

'I believe you are right, Macarthur. I believe you to be right. But what to do?'

Marshall turned to both men, fully, a blaze in his eye.

'I shall not traverse that path – no, sir, not in such weather. Edinburgh be damned!'

'I will do it. Inspect matters, for all of us,' said Macarthur, evenly. He stood serene, several fathoms up from the calm bubble of his words.

'Are ye sure, Donald?' said Ducat. 'I should remain to – well, to document, all that you find.'

He cut his eyes away without revealing their contents.

'I understand, sir. I understand.'

*

At the bent railings Macarthur paused, taking hold of what grip nature had left him, then turned to look behind. His two colleagues had dwindled already – their heads seemed smaller, necks elongated, their bodies shrinking back from the cliff-edge as though at the site of some horrible outbreak of disease. Macarthur shook his own, to further clear his vision, but this odd perspective remained.

No matter.

Onwards.

He tried, in turning, not to think of any kind of thanks – the pleasure of the Board at a hard but necessary job, well done, perhaps a letter of commendation in his file; but more than this, the gratitude of the two men receding from his sight, the knowledge that he was a true keeper. It was easy to forget, for in mounting the edge, he disappeared into quite another world entirely.

Here, step by treacherous step, the cliff's splintered teeth pushed forward, spiked as the serried ranks of a shark's fearsome jaws, to catch and seize and slice him clean in two. The wind rose beyond all imagining, wilder than a pack of dogs maddened by thirst, heavier than the beasts on his grandmother's farm, startled by a gun in the farmyard and stampeding pell-mell towards him, a hundred tonnes of death rolling down the incline. But cows he could see. The wind's stiff haunches coiled and sprang, sprang and coiled, only to attack with fingers tipped with invisible, icy talons. Inside his oily hood he cried out, yet – once again – it was a faint, transitory horror. He felt warm with the knowledge of good, and urged his battered limbs on stair by jagged stair.

Halfway down. The ocean, opening before him, wore the blackest and most forbidding aspect he had ever seen: here, a hundred feet below, bruised and columned, rising and falling with the devil's energy, it smacked the dock like a punch-drunk fighter too far gone to know the round was over, pounding all in sight with insane unstoppable fury.

There, further out where ordinarily one might see the *Hesperus*'s glad bobbing shape round the bay, were only great staggering walls of black water, so high no cresting foam tipped their limits. He had visited Edinburgh, once – it was enough, even in memory – and wandered through the high-stacked monstrous tenements of the Old Town. Their crusted, yawning walls overhung everything, much like these towers of dark water, but with this exception: none was moving in, remorselessly, to crush each living thing in their implacable claws.

Nonetheless, huddled around this newfound warmth of spirit, Macarthur pressed on. Here and there were scrags of metal and old rope, severed and flung about; round each step the encircling grass was so sodden it shone like a hangman's rope, hosed for the drop. He advanced in a wobble-and-shuffle, half crouched like the crab, calves and forearms burning with living, crawling cramp. Now he was near, and taking a moment to breathe, he turned to look around. All must be surveyed, Donald, he told himself; all catalogued, though the circumstances of such an audit felt like taking tally in the madhouse when the inmates had been loosed upon the asylum.

Looking forward, he saw the tackle-box had been torn from its frame and dashed against the rocks, but miraculously remained within the bay, splintered corners intact but bruised with smutches of seaweed. Ropes from inside had uncoiled and were strewn over several rocks, their ends moving ominously across the swirling black surface. Here, too, was the life ring – how absurdly jaunty, how reminiscent of a sane world, were its fat red and white stripes! – flung a hundred feet from one side of the bay to the other, impaled upon a spur of snapped railing. Fresh metal protruded through the canvas like bone through a trouser leg. It trailed its own rope in the waters, crossing now and again, as unseen currents twined about, with the tackle ropes. The landside rocket was nowhere to be seen, sucked away to the depths, he presumed.

He surveyed the scene rapidly, his mind (how sweetly it seemed to be working! as smooth as oil) cataloguing all, both present and missing, in its current position. He felt within the small oval of his oilskin that the end of the world might be similarly marked down, by those recording angels his grandmother spoke of; unseen, yes, but poised over every scene of human endeavour with quills to hand, ready to observe and take down, and present at the last trump with all the solidity of fact.

Done, he turned back to face the cliff. The water behind him, thick with rope and vast weighty substance, rolled and stirred. But Macarthur would not see. Now, in his bones, came flashes of sudden, undeniable heat: a warming, stirring, a burning of roots from the inside out, as though some maiden lay peeling his outer skin away to reveal a new inner glory. He held up one hand in the raging spume, looked on in awe, flung away his glove.

From above came shouts or raving seagulls; he knew not, nor cared. For the hand before him was a skeleton-work of electric blue: bones, veins, sinew, all lit with some undying fire, of sapphire or lapis lazuli, that seemed to infuse the entire bay and come streaming like beneficent light down from it, through it, only to blaze out again in his fingertips. He gasped. Now his arm, his legs and torso, even face could he have seen blazing blue with preternatural light. He did not understand, and found with relief he did not wish to. In his ecstasy he found some redemption, beyond ordinary hopes of day-to-day-success, the praise of the Edinburgh high heed-yins or his family's knowledge of his elevated status, at last. He wished to share this high blue joy with his comrades.

He belched, and in the sudden, earthy eructation – redolent of rye, and underneath, some rotten fungal thing, its fingers tickling his throat – came his last taste of earth. He looked heavenwards, raised electric arms.

But where he expected two small, human dots – blips of oil two hundred feet up – he saw instead, on bolts of white flashing, two great muscled creatures surfing and leaping down the cliff as though skipping down a burn.

Afraid, he stepped back, feet one step closer to the sucking edge.

What were they? He held out his hands, beseeching; rubbed his eyes, waited as the rain lashed, the sea spray rasped about his ears, for words of greeting, for the resolution of this nightmarish shift to known and friendly men, bent on his same mission.

But the creatures came on.

Two there were, no more – but of what size! Almost as tall as the water, and just as blue – now blue, now black, now crested with rippling furls like weed or scales – as they stormed past rail and flushed across the last steps, the rugged stone of the dock. He stepped back again. To Macarthur's eyes, they were immense, giants of wave and tempest; he himself shrank down, into the blue, craving only light and safety. The creatures reared above him, ribbed chests frantic with barnacles and tangled weed. It rotted through their muscles like ingrown hair, snarled about their arms and great hooked fingers like long-drowned locks, the rank tresses of the merman.

What were they? In God's name, what!

But from his grandmother's fireplace came the knowledge. Sprites, of water – horses, when they chose, to ride the wavetops; men, when they so desired, to clasp and tangle the unwary mariner in their rhymes and hooks. Yet these towering beasts did not speak, made no song nor dalliance with meter. Instead they rose, ever taller, glaring about and down as though masters of all they saw, and he the least, most miserable speck of all in their terrible vision.

'What do you want?' he screamed into the wind.

But they came on, implacable as the highest tenement, dripping slime and shell and wild weed about their foul-maned heads. He trembled backwards one more step, felt the blunted edge of the dock crumble beneath his heel. Macarthur looked up, cricking his neck, to the ripped black towers of horror looming above him, and felt the crack and disintegration of smashed wood behind him, the sudden reach of black water, then a thousand prickling fingers as it engulfed his flailing body.

A great arch of water joined over him, and the heat burned out of his limbs. He looked back at the blue kelpies rearing over the dock and saw in their ragged arms the lifting intent to follow, one after the other, faces gaunt and lit by horror-light and the mad wash of the storm.

Was there to be no end!

But soon the black arch folded over his starting eyes. Lifting his limp form onto a rolling stack, the ocean enfolded the dock and sucked him away to eternity, while the storm beat on as though wound to fever, its clockwork mangled but running still, ticking loud and bleak against sky and depthless churn, pulling in first one shivering, shrieking figure, then the other, then the railing, the shattered dock, the ropes and the mystery and everything else under the empty cliff.

Something More Than Night

Black Mask characters lived in a world gone wrong, a world in which, long before the atom bomb, civilization had created the machinery for its own destruction … The streets were dark with something more than night

Raymond Chandler, Introduction to *The Smell of Fear*

'LEMME GET this straight, Monica – just so's I understand.'

She nodded, her kohl-rimmed eyes wide and frank.

'Okay – yeah, Ray. What dontcha unnerstand?'

'You took this message for me while I was out. About a job, seemingly.'

'Yeah.'

'And this mystery man offering a job – no company, or whatnot – but the job would be worth my while. Is that it?'

'Yeah. Worth your while, that was what the guy said. I wrote it down, see.'

She displayed a notepad from the LA Creamery on the breakfast-nook. They were giving them away when you added any item to your usual order. Clotted cream, in our case. It said *worth wile* in her rounded, little-girl handwriting. She tapped the page.

'And this man also just happened, without saying his own name, to mention the title of the series I've been working on. That he liked my work. The secret, *illegal* series.'

'*Saucy Secrets*, yeah. That's what he said.'

I took a minute to mull over what she was saying – what the guy was saying, I suppose, whoever the hell he might be. I picked up the notepad and looked over the proposed place and time: *Bradbry Bldg, dusk.* I picked it up, used a corner to scratch the wild itch that had broken out on my neck. It was maybe just crazy enough to be true.

'Alright, doll,' I said, and kissed her.

*

I had a few things to do before I could head downtown to the meet. Not least, the latest instalment of my series in *Saucy Secrets*, the erotic adventures of one Delilah McTavish ("Nails your balls to the wall, then drains you dry!"). This month, Delilah was turning her attention to the ladies, setting up a false store-front to tout silk stockings at cotton prices, with comfortable sectioned benches and beefcake assistants to speed things along. Five minutes after the inevitable ruckus, the benches tipped back and hey presto – Sweeney Todd! But that was just my mind making itself feel better. The degenerates on Al's sheet – who didn't seem to mind their names appearing on a circulation list, even if Al swore up and down it never left the safe – weren't too particular about *denouements*, character, even the story itself. Fightin, feelin and fuckin; that was more their style, and I had rent to pay, a girl to keep happy. Some of them could barely read, but it was a whole lot easier to hide your printed smut from the prying eyes of the wife or girlfriend. Naked pictures were a harder sell. Even in this tawdry tale, there it is: the *double entendre*. These mutts hardly had a single entendre, but Monica ain't living on cottage cheese.

I'd come to this sloppy, moralising burg five years before to make my mark at the *Times*, or the *Daily News*, at least. Couple years on the school paper and a taste for the racier kind of magazine propelled me to the heart of the city, but those lofty assholes weren't buying. Too regional, they said, or not enough experience; or, more memorably, fuck off, kid. That one I stuck in my scrapbook.

So I knocked around writing this and that for the free-sheets, and humped crates out back of the Creamery to make ends meet. Monica might spoon that clotted shit on her taters like there's no tomorrow, but I won't touch the stuff. Not after seeing a crateful bloat out on the loading dock through one long summer afternoon.

Anyways, Al shuffles these funny little circulars all round the neighbourhoods. Coupons, mostly, but enough filler so some desperate hack's needed to pad out the offers with local news, pig-roasts, kewpie dolls and all that. He could see I had an eye for detail.

'Hey, Ray,' he says one morning – well, noon; Al doesn't do mornings – 'nice work on that carnival thing. Ferris wheel, shooting ranges – good stuff. Keepin the housewives happy!'

He's not normally this talkative till he's dropped a slug of rye into the first of his many cups of coffee. Proceed with caution.

'Yeah? You gonna need me any more this week, only I'd like to take Monica down – '

'Na. Not news, anyways. Listen. You gotta good eye, I know that. You ain't queer, are ya?'

'What?'

'Simmer down – I don't mean nothin by it. I don't care what a guy gets up to on his own time, anyway, but what I mean is, I gotta – uh, gottan opportunity for the right guy who knows how to use his peepers, can sorta translate it all nice an spicy on the page. Guy who knows how to ogle the ladies, ya know. A *guy*.'

I had a few things to say about this – not least I'd just mentioned Monica, and not for the first time – but suddenly the moist, greasy smell of money was in the air.

'A guy, okay. I'm listening.'

'Yeah, you get it. So, here's the thing – ya know who consumes these free-sheets?'

'Sure – housewives, folks with an interest in what's going on in the city – *their* part of the city, anyway – and maybe like a good deal, now and again. Salta-the-earth types.'

'Yeah, okay Ray. But you know where the money *ain't*, and that's in salt.'

I must have looked confused. One of the office boys came in looking for an address, and Al sent him out with a flea in his ear. He flipped the Do Not Disturb sign, cranked the blinds till they snapped shut like the clasp on a miser's purse, and sighed.

'Don't get me wrong,' Al said, 'I don't have nuthin against anyone takes one of our rags. The more the merrier. *He* loved 'em.'

He jerked an inky, well-chewed thumb over one shoulder at the photograph of his old man, patriarch and founder of the firm. 'So I guess I love 'em, too. Keeps things ticking over. But it ain't what you'd call the kinda material to get a man up outta bed in the mornin, if ya take my drift. I don't sit up and beg for coupons. And if I'm right about you, kewpie-dolls don't do it for you, neither.'

I wasn't much more enlightened than when we started in on this little tete-a-tete, but the greasy smell lingered on, beyond the office boy and the blinds. I'd been known to sit up and beg for that.

'Alright, Al – I'll bite. I'm a red-blooded American male. Now what are ya drivin at?'

He shifted some considerable weight from one haunch to the other, so he could reach down into the leg-hole of the desk. I heard a fat click, the sort the peeper hears when a bright boy gets the drop on him in one of the pulps, only it was a secret door unlatching, not the click of a hammer. I shifted about a bit, to see if I could catch a glimpse of what was down there. Hollow panel, I thought; maybe a safe.

'Wrap your eyes round that.'

I stared, then caught a guffaw in my throat and quickly strangled it down to a cough. I'd seen this kind of shit before, handed round the schoolyard ten years before: Ignatz giving Krazy a bone instead of a brick; Felix the Cat, up to dickens with his big, jolly hands; even Mickey schtupping a frankly none-too-reluctant Minnie, by the end. The effect was determined entirely by how long the 'artist' spent goofing off in woodshop – most looked little better than jerky stick figures, with a characteristic blob here or there to denote character. I took the magazine between pinched fingers, as though picking up a roach.

But when I looked, flicked quickly through the crisp pages, it wasn't that at all.

Saucy Secrets, the thing said, over a painted mouth hinting at those selfsame secrets. There were no pictures, and the thing was neatly and professionally laid out, on thick stock, with chapters and little potted biographies of the writers in fine italic at the end. I assumed the contributors were pseudonyms, and Al confirmed it.

'Not that I wouldn't put my own name against any of these pieces, you understand,' he said, leaning over and tapping one, 'A Pound of Flesh', by Philip McCann. 'This here's top-quality stuff. But my *name*, you know – it ain't the same as ladies' marketing.'

I flipped to the end. The shell-pink endpapers were smooth and plain, and there was nothing on the back cover, not even a price.

'Where – I mean, *how* d'you sell this stuff, Al?'

'Sells itself.'

'Yeah, I'm sure.' I wasn't sure what kind of writing was sandwiched between the creamy covers, but was pretty sure it would indeed move just fine on its own.

'Only I don't exactly sell it – this is more of a rental-type operation. No price, and it ain't because it's priceless. My man with the press prints up a hundred of each, tops, and I keep a list of who's got what, and when they're due back. Nice and clean, on subscription, one copy of the distribution list, everybody's happy.'

'So why'd you need me?'

'McCann croaked, and I can't write for shit.'

I sat back for a minute with the magazine in my lap. It had a pleasing heft, left no ink on my palms or the edge of my cuffs. It still gave off that heady waft of grease, along with the sour, electric undercurrent of the truly shady.

'How much per piece?' He named a figure.

I started the next morning.

*

First things first. The Olds was thirsty – it was always thirsty – but had nothing in the tank. I had to fill up, and now was as good a time as any. If I had to stop by the gas station, it could never be when I had Monica along for the ride. She hated them.

'I don't like waiting at gas stations – you know that, Ray.'

Yeah; I knew. I just didn't understand. I always liked them: the smooth transition from light to shadow, tyres dinging the pipe and bringing out the guy from some bay in back (where doubtless he was working on his boss's ride); joshing with the pump-jockey, taking that lordly tone when you told him to fill her up; the riff of crisp bills as you stuffed the cash into his hand, that little chipper wave on the way out. What was her problem? But she sat there like a jester at a funeral every damn time.

For some reason the jockey was taking his time, though I'd made a good long ding, so I stepped away from the pumps to light a smoke. I unfolded Monica's note again, wondering what I was getting into. This guy hadn't set off any bells for her, but that didn't mean it was A-okay to just pass it on. For starters, what did the guy mean, at dusk? I'd taken the trouble to check up on sunsets in my *Farmer's Almanac* – you never can tell what sort of weird shit these rustic guys need to know – and according to Old Clem, dark would fall tonight around eight. I checked my watch; six thirty. If the jockey would hurry up, I'd time for a cup of coffee and a hamburger before heading downtown.

But why dusk? Did this guy sprout hair and teeth when the moon came up, or what? More likely he wore them out and proud as he went about his shady business, in this city. Also, how exactly did he know about *Saucy Secrets*? Al kept that list locked up tighter than the queen's thighs. I scratched my head with the end of the match, dropped it in the ashcan. What the hell – it might be interesting just to see the guy's face, and there's often a story in the murkiest corners. Those preachy old pricks with the *Times* wouldn't know that if it bit them in the ass.

At the Bay City Diner, Maureen was working, thank God. I can front it out with the best in the business, but even I need a friendly face sometimes, a good dose of grease to tamp down the butterflies, meeting a new client.

'Ray,' she said, already pouring.

'Doll. How's things? Walter alright?'

'So-so, darlin, okay. Can't ask much more than that. Usual?'

Ordinarily, I take my hamburger on the rare side, with a lightly-toasted bun and a heap of fiery onions that have barely kissed the grill, but a pile of caustic rings didn't seem like the best idea for my mystery evening.

'Not tonight – tell Ruff to hold the onions, maybe slip in a slice of tomato or two.'

'You got it.'

I was halfway through the burger (not bad), when it occurred to me Maureen was free and easy with her opinions, and had some life experience, into the bargain; it was written on her face, the gnarls and colours of the back of her hands, too, the first time she tipped a coffee pot in my direction. She came for a refill and I touched her hand. Nice and light; nothing too forward.

'Yeah, hon?'

'Maureen, you know any reason why a man might wanna meet for business in the evening, at dusk specifically?'

She rocked back on her heels for a second. The coffee rimmed the glass bowl, doing a slow roll up to the lip then back while she thought, but not a drop spilled.

'Well, yeah.'

'Like what?'

'You really wanna know?'

'Sure I do. Wouldn't've asked if I didn't.'

'Well, okay. I can think of a couple – suming your guy's a real businessman, ya know, and not some crook.'

'Oh, he's real,' I replied, with a magnificent confidence I surely did not possess.

'Well, some businesses run at night, you know. Take this here. I do the occasional night shift when Clara's off – she seems to run into a lotta door-frames, ya know – an it's completely different to days. Different feel, different folks. Different priorities, see. I don't mind, but Clara when she's on, she loves it. Wouldn't wanna work no other way. Maybe your guy's like that.'

'He works in the Bradbury.'

'That big ol place downtown?'

'Yeah, that's the one. No offence, but it might not work quite the same way as this wonderful diner of yours.'

She gave me the stink-eye, switched the pot to her other hand.

'What's the other reason?'

'You won't laugh?'

'I dunno – is it funny? I might.'

'You laugh, an Monica'll be cookin those burgers of yours from now on.'

'Alright – alright. I won't laugh. What you got?'

'Well, my uncle ...'

She trailed off, casting a look around the diner. Her load was light this evening – she had only me and a couple of driving-types, a bit rough around the edges, in her section. They were knee-deep in beef. With a last glance at the kitchen, she eased her butt onto the back brace of my booth, took off a load.

'My uncle, he was a bit – different. Even from a child he was always sniffin an snifflin – dogs, cats, horses, dander, everythin that shed would set him off. Couldn't stand dust, or shrimp. He was a mess. They had him tested an all, but nothin seemed to be it. Then one summer they kept him in, so's the pollen wouldn't get him, ya know, and it was a scorcher. They wrapped the house up tight and waited it out. But you know what?'

I'd heard some tales, but this one took the ribbon.

'What?'

'After a week in the dark, he was fine. I mean, not just *not bad*, actually *fine* – skippin about like a spring lamb, breathin wonderful, happy as a pig in shit.'

'So what was it?'

'Light!'

'What! That's the stupidest thing I ever heard.'

'I swear. He was allergic to light. Got himself through high school, into night school to learn his trade, an only works nights – ever. Still going strong, eighty five. Don't see him much, bein dayshift, you know, but still. Weirdest thing I ever saw.'

I took a long sip of coffee and shook my head.

'How rare would you say this thing is your uncle has, Maureen? It common?'

'Only case I ever heard of.'

'And your uncle, he never bumped into anyone else with it – at the hospital, maybe, or the carnival?'

'Hey! That's Wilbur you're talkin bout. You want me to refresh that?'

'Yeah, sure. Got a few things to think about.'

'Alright, darlin. You chew em over and I'll get you fixed up.'

After three cups, an hour bumper-to-bumper getting downtown, I was none the wiser. Still, old Wilbur was going strong, and that was the main thing.

*

The Bradbury was supposed to be something else, and from the outside it looked nice enough – sort of toned-down fancy, with sandstone wings wrapping around the block – but inside it seemed pokey, even cramped. I handed over the note to the man at the desk. *MC* was all it had identifying this mystery businessman and I expected a ruckus to even get in, but the guy had to suppress a yawn as he bumped up the bill of his braided cap for a scratch.

'Oh, yuh – he's on five. Strange kinda fella. No trouble, mind you.'

He pointed out a bend and staircase back over his shoulder, then went back to his comic book.

'I don't need a badge or anything?'

The man at the desk shook his head, so I took him at his word. These millionaire types – you'd think having spent so much on a building, they'd throw a few dollars at security, too. I followed my nose down the narrow alley of the lobby and took the stairs. It was dusk here, alright, under the low electric light of a single globe, then full-on night as

I came up into a huge atrium. There was wood and cast-iron everywhere. It looked as though I could get up to five by way of a series of rising half-stairs. As I went up, the light softened – broadened – till it felt like fairyland. From the top I had a look over the balustrade, but it was just me enjoying the view. The first corridor, on the right, didn't give up its secrets. The second had a bar of brilliance spilling over tile at the far end. I squared my shoulders and headed that way.

The door was half-open, propped against an iron boot-scraper in the shape of a lion rampant. I stepped around it, knocked sharply. The sound reverberated through the wood, and seemingly the empty quiet of the whole building. Where was everybody?

'Hello there? Calling on a job. Raymond Tapley!'

Inside, nothing changed – the illumination from the hanging globes didn't waver; no secretary, earning that pay-check, crooked an elegant neck from the inner sanctum to bid me welcome – but a voice emerged from somewhere by the windows, or so I assumed. It was a masculine voice, yet held the crystalline, tinkling sweetness of a mountain stream. It did not boom, but the glass bowls of the hanging globes positively quivered at its vibrations.

'Enter,' the voice said, 'and bring a little of your magic with your will.'

'Hello?'

I stepped inside. There was a slight rush of air as I walked across the threshold, and a globe above the empty reception desk buzzed briefly. It was a nice office; a *nice* office. Beyond the desk, at the end of a long runner decorated with curling briars and heraldic beasts, stood the largest grandfather clock I had ever seen. Behind it was an enormous plate glass window covered in closed, lustrous wooden blinds. They looked like teak. The whole place was panelled, too, in deep ebony tones, with every second panel inlaid with horned talons, peaks of jagged mountains and dragons in repeating patterns. Who was this guy?

From another door, placed where the runner stopped, the voice came again.

'Please, enter.'

I did.

Inside was brilliant – scintillating, coruscating; blazing with electric light. He had added three more ceiling-globes, and each surface was crusted with lanterns like barnacles clinging to a celestial boat. The man sat, back to the door, facing a marble fireplace in which a fire roared – in July! – adding further shifting lustre to every surface. Even from behind, where I could see only the crown of his thick black hair, he seemed large. As he rose and turned, I had to stifle a gasp. This fella was huge! Gigantic – six eight, six ten at least, and solid as a battering ram, or a gargoyle carved for the ages, hanging off the side of some French cathedral.

He bowed, extended a sweeping arm in welcome. His face came down from craggy heights, peaked hairline savage as an axe-edge, to a sharp, noble chin. The cheekbones sang like sirens, bracketing a bladelike nose which cast shadows of its own. The eyes were pools of pitch, the mouth creased up in a startling imitation of a smile, revealing nothing. I nodded, knock-kneed as a first grader. My mouth, usually quite confident, twitched and spasmed like a handful of chewed cotton as the summer flames crackled madly on.

'I – ah, well. I came like you said. Dusk, though I gotta say it ain't too dusky in here.'

He smiled again, turned, walked over to the blinds. My buttocks unclenched a fraction as my brain scrambled for purchase on the bleak, slippery rockface. His next words were a surprise.

'You are a writer, yes?'

I agreed. I don't recall whether I nodded or spoke, but he got the message.

'Then where are your writing materials?'

I am not a stupid guy, at least I don't think so. Monica might not agree, or Maureen on a bad day, but now my tongue felt like a chewtoy, the mind behind it shocked and stupefied into silence. Yet it wasn't dull – instead of the grey matter striving for a *bon mot*, there was alarm in my tissues, a cry of shock standing straight like an enormous exclamation mark stuck in the meat of my brain. I could feel this man's presence grubbing up the edges of my mind, feeling for an entry point, working its way in. I shook my head and bit down hard. Come on, Ray. This is a job; nothing more.

'Listen,' I said, 'you know my name, but I don't know yours.'

'My name is Carpathian.'

'Oh yeah? Carpathian what?'

The man shifted his bulk in the direction of the fire and made a small crooked smile before turning to face the flames.

'Carpathian is my family name. For the moment, I have chosen a more – fitting first name, for my current profession, in this locale.'

'And it begins with 'M'?'

'Indeed. Do you need to know so much about each potential employer, Mr Tapley? I am familiar with your work, and it is this familiarity which has drawn you to me.'

I could feel this thing slipping away.

'Well, no, Mr Carpathian, I don't suppose I need to know much more than that. You know my work, you say? You mentioned *Saucy Secrets* to my lady friend. You mind telling me exactly how you knew about that?'

'I know of many things in this country. I have been here … for some while, though I do not come from America originally, but rather a different country. I know, for example, that American men have an itch which cannot be scratched.'

Ha! A zinger from the great aristocratic galoot looming over his roaring fire like a moose busting down a barn-door!

'Alright. That, I grant you. But howd'ya get a hold of it in the first place?'

'I visited Mr Shaker one evening. He and I had a most illuminating conversation.'

'I'll bet. And you just happened to come away with a copy, and in that copy, you spotted my work?'

'Just so. The delectable Miss McTavish.'

'Alright. Listen, can I sit?'

'Please.'

He turned back to me, indicated another tall-backed chair fringing the hearth. I sat down and he sat back into his own.

'So, you mentioned a job. What's on your mind?'

'Tell me, Mr Tapley, how it feels to sink your teeth into a scene?'

'Pardon me?'

'I believe that is how writers describe an absorbing job of writing, is it not? Almost as a meal, a steak upon which the mind feeds?'

'Well, yeah, I suppose so.'

'So describe it. Please.'

Again with the gesturing arm, heavy, smooth as a crane against the skyline. Only this one had long fingers tipped with pointy nails instead of a hook. I thought for a minute, moving my hat-brim through my fingers in a chain of little twitches.

'Okay – well, suppose you wanna start a story – a news-piece, say, or a feature. You don't wanna sit down at the typewriter and roll in a fresh sheet of paper. There's nothing scarier than that.'

He nodded, slightly but perceptibly. Alright.

'So, before you put your tush on that seat – long before – you need something that gets your blood going. An idea, a feeling, a sense of character, somewhere or somebody.'

'Like Miss McTavish.'

'Exactly! Now, see, when Al – uh, Mr Shaker – when Al first approached me about this … line of work, he wasn't real specific about what he wanted. In fact, he was a bit like a blank sheet himself. Just get me hard, was his drift. But what I like is soft – hard don't do it. You can keep your rock-hard jocks, your sweaty beefcakes digging up the highway; not interested. But *soft* – that's somewhere to start. Round, succulent, curvy. Mobile, you know. And *then* I wondered what you might get if you had the nicest, juiciest exterior, but an inside flinty as any man you've ever met. That might work.'

'So. We have your blood moving, as you say. Where then?'

'Well, Mr Carpathian, then you put your ass down in fronta that bastard thirsty white page, and get started. I like to think of it like this: nobody eats a huge meal in one go, am I right? You get your horse doovers first, soup or whatnot; then your main; then your dessert, if you're so inclined, with maybe a bottle of something alongside. Only trenchermen slam it all down in one go. And that's how the brain works, too, least mine does. Little, juicy pieces.'

'I am a large man, Mr Tapley. Why would I not start in immediately, as your trencherman might?'

'Well, see, you could; I won't argue with you there. But even as a – uh, a larger fellow, say, why'd you want to? Just because something's hard – and there's nothing harder than sitting down in front of those arctic wastes, specially with some editor expecting you to paint a penguin – it doesn't mean it ain't worth doing well. I do it in little sips.'

'Sips?'

'Yeah, sips. So your penguin, see, he don't appear on the page all at once, flippers and what have you. He comes about slowly, in his own way. What I mean is, start the meal gradual. Feel your way in. Maybe it's a snow drift, and he thought when he went off to fish out some mackerel for the missus that he'd left her safely behind. Maybe he gets back, fish in flipper, and instead of the drift there's a big crack in the ice. No missus, and suddenly the ground's a bit shaky. Now what if he jumps off that piece of 'berg at the last minute, crawls out the other side and sees his lady away in the distance. She's saved! But wait, there's a polar bear coming up behind! You see what I'm saying? Little pieces, right off the side. When you do that, you getta steak by the end your teeth are goin to remember.'

Carpathian sat back in his chair, tenting his fingers like the rafters of some ancient church. After an eternity he smiled.

'I believe I do see, yes, Mr Tapley. And Miss McTavish?'

'Same deal, cept she's a hot piece, not a chilly animal. I don't hold with animals, anyhow. Hold up the story. That's the main thing – I figure you want me for the story, right? Gotta bit of trouble at night, can't quite see to Mrs Carpathian right, you know? Need some spice?'

'*No!*'

Carpathian roared and the fire leapt up as if in response. I jerked back, shocked at the sudden force. I raised my hands.

'Hey, man – Mr Carpathian, I'm sorry. I didn't mean to offend you, or your good lady wife. I mean – '

He waved me away as he might a troublesome fly.

'It is nothing. But there is no *Mrs* Carpathian, nor am I troubled by any sluggishness of the blood. I wish to employ you for something far more important.'

Slowly he stood, reaching his full height, and blocking half the light from the leaping flames. I looked up at him in awe. The blades of his face sharpened as he drew back his lips, ran long tapering fingers through his hair. He bent his face to mine, eyes wolf-wide, and spoke so softly I could barely make him out.

'I wish you,' he said, 'to write my story.'

*

'As I have said, Mr Tapley, I do not come from this great country. I do not come from this continent, or from this time. Do you notice my voice? It is warm, commanding – perhaps also a touch frightening? It is so. I see a tremble in your fingers. Dispel such cowardice. A man who can conceive the depraved adventures of Miss McTavish cannot be threatened by such cold realities. Take up that pencil, this notebook. That is good.

'I do not come from your land, but another, from a time far beyond the span of your life. Carpathian is a name, but not my name. It is the name of my home. My first name, *Marvin*, I chose as typical of your country, but I do not use it often. If I must, with my few superiors in the Syndicate, I will allow it to pass their lips, but it means nothing – a mere flickering of lights. If we succeed, Mr Tapley, you may know my real name. I notice your hand flying across paper. This is good, but is not necessary. Listen alone; the record will take care of itself.

'I arrived on these shores more than thirty years ago. I had experienced some – difficulties, shall we say, in my homeland, from a band of inquisitive fellows with too much time, and too little learning. My gypsies were not equal to the task, so I repelled these boarders myself, and drank my victory in their blood. But for a time I must move on.

'Where on the great spinning globe should I go, where make a new home? Which land thirsted for those things I myself craved, which offered sanctuary to a poor yet unvanquished soul? As I passed from countryside to city, under cover of night, I heard one peasant talk of some beverage, Coca-Cola, newly arrived in the city.

'"Not want for stimulation, with such a brew!" he said to his companion, in our language, you understand. They stood in the slit-mouth of an alley by the drinking quarter. I had found refreshment there myself, from time to time. He tipped a bottle, smacked his lips. The other snatched it away.

'I heard of this again and again in the days that followed. I noticed, also, products of different kinds had come to my land from yours. Things which needed not language to cross borders, but which tapped into baser needs. Cigarettes. Frontier liquor. A moment before I departed, sure this new insatiable land was my destination, came those flickering, herky-jerky films for which your town is famed.

'This country, Mr Tapley, has a great many thirsts, and a great many liquids with which to quench them.

'In the drinking quarter, also, I found a man able to craft the documents I would require. What need have I for papers, lord of a thousand years over every man, woman and child? But your customs are not mine, and he was able – if perhaps not willing – to work until the sun came up. I left, after sating myself, the papers in my possession.

'So. You have me then at point of departure: a proud man, stripped by savages of his birth right, yet not entirely powerless in the swirling currents of a new age. Those things which I have were fitted perfectly for this new world. I took passage in a steamer, walked the decks at dusk to clear both mind and palette, then docked at New York after a most satisfactory period at sea.

'But where to go? I did not require assistance with my baggage, for I brought none, and walked instead down the teeming arteries of the city as the sun ran cold and the gutters steamed. Nothing – no man of this land – could stop my passage.

'Your country holds a great many charms for those from an older place. The sparkle of glass, tall and uncorrupted in the reflected glow of dying light; the reach of vast buildings, sheer and violent as impossible cliffs; the mingling of so many souls it is fruitless to count them. Where a man has money the land is rich with gifts. Where he has none, it is barren, so each man seeks pleasures where he is able. In New York, it seemed, such bursts of happiness leapt up most often from the silvered screen.

'I came upon a theatre on Broadway as a man was opening his kiosk and extending a bright canvas awning across the street.

'"What is this, playing this evening, sir?' I asked. I had not yet the fluency of English, and sounded doubtless as a foreigner might.

'Finest show in the world!' he replied. 'Comedy! Tragedy! All the splendour of the fair, at a fraction of the price! Ten cents.'

'"But what is this movie?'

'"Oh, sorry bub. 'The Lucky Dog'. Not bad.'

'So I gave him a coin and entered. Inside was a large, ornate theatre not unlike those of my homeland, which made a study of penny operas and cheap melodrama. Where, I was sure, the stage had been instead was a large flat screen of painted canvas. It was ugly beside the moulded plaster flowers and shining boards. But no matter – a moment after and all conversation ceased; the beams sprang up before the crowd. I had no interest in this tale of two idiots, or for that matter any human tale, so I watched instead the faces of the crowd: blade-cheeked young men stuffing in candy; plump matrons, shocked then pleased in turn; prim young women in floppy hats, their gloved hands rising and falling to the mad thumping of the idiot on the piano. All life seemed to be here. But I was interested in three things. That the antics of the idiots enthralled them, yes. Such is relief from life's pressures, I suppose. I have always taken relief elsewhere.

'But also, Mr Tapley, a fascination with light. I could see it on every face, the way each lit up when the sun threw down its awful sparkle and shadow. The smile of recognition, of need, at its power in the dust, even the suggestion of bright water. This I noted keenly. And lastly, for all their awkward progress, the awe of the automobile. Perhaps this New York crowd needed not a personal mode of travel in their crowded, horse-filled city. But still, that slight intake of breath when the machine kicked and burped across the screen. This, also, I noted.

'It was not a long movie, and I had no heart for the others that followed. I considered loitering in the exit tunnel, where I had sought sustenance at other times, other cities. But such was the power of the spindly beams, and the fascination their images worked on humanity, that I could not linger. I had much to think on.

'I must think, and so I walked.

'As with your routine for writing – small bites, big steaks, and so on and so forth – I too must plan my life if it is to be a success. Or this much I thought when I was coming to your country. I find since I arrived, and most particularly since I moved to California, the dreadful land of light, that all is the big steak: there is less room, and indeed less need, for the small and cautious bite. But pay no heed. Since time out of mind, if I have had to think, I have walked.

'It was no matter to stride the length of Manhattan island, and I did it. From top to bottom, high park and dense tenement, to promenade and water was a mere moment, but in my night passage my mind raced faster than any leg. Yes, this teeming island was a paradise for one of my kind. It had dark corners, stuffed with life; great towers of flesh and blood rising upwards forever, with nary a glance between neighbours; alleys rife with darkness, and food which would never be missed by anyone. The city, too, swirled with balmy cloud and ice for half the year. It was inexhaustible. And yet …

'Those faces caught in the beams, Mr Tapley! Such worship of light, so beneficent and health-giving to them! What a meal they would make. And mobile, loose, disconnected – jetting about here and there in their puttering metal insects, drinking the ancient lifeblood of the earth as though it were so much water! It was clear to California I must go. Yet how to reach this oil-soaked nirvana, and once there, how survive – for both money (as they recognise no royalty but stick-figures on a screen) and against sun? No matter. Another circuit of that rich-veined island, and I had made my plan.'

*

So far, he'd talked like a freight train under a full head of steam. Measured and purposeful, yes, with that odd honeyed accent – the words biting like steel underneath – but bulleting along as though cranked from the barrel of a Gatling gun. My hand was warm, fingers knotted. I could barely keep up, instructions be damned.

'How are you going on with your notes, Mr Tapley?'

I jerked my head up, arrested by the direct address. Each time he had mentioned my name in the flow of his story it felt rhetorical, as though I stood in for all of my fellow Americans, or none, if he was directing his ire in my particular direction.

'Um, okay, I guess? Keeping up. I had a few – '

'That is good. Now to where my story truly begins.'

*

'"Yes, if you please," I said to the workman. "Simply make the crate whole, then seal it."

'"Seal it, sir?"

'"Yes."

'"But there's yet nothing in it!"

'"That, my good man, is none of your concern."

'I waited until the fellow had made an excellent job: stout wood, cross-bracing, rivets the size of a man's knuckles. He sealed it fully, then I finished him for his inquisitiveness and dropped his empty body from the dock. I slid between two cross-braces like a sea fog, then awaited lading and the long rest as my train rattled across the country. No light pierced the seals; I had a most pleasant journey.

'In San Francisco, I was not long delayed. After a brief stroll up the hills, I whispered back into the crate for its onward passage to Los Angeles, your fair city. It was not so long back – five years, at most. A mere spark in the furnace of history. Yet what a period it was! The acme of motion pictures, blossoming into full reproduction of the moving world, with sound and all its resonant qualities! Citrus bursting the seams of the state. A massive oil boom, and the blessed dominance of the automobile. You may smile, sir, at such a word, but even such as I can feel the blessing of the universe. Think on it: a million years in the making, and when human technology wakes to the power of long-stored energy – positively *drinks* it in, Mr Tapley! – why there it sits beneath the ground at your feet, pregnant with force, waiting simply to be released, the perfect match of circumstance and opportunity.

'And yet, one small problem remained. Not travel – sufficient lubrication of the wheels, here and there, and my crate was delivered intact and at dusk to a crumbling mansion on Fairfax. No, I speak of sunlight and its – deleterious effects. Let me save your laughter. Why sail for a new world saturated in sun, you may ask yourself? And once there, why sail from a world of high and low seasons, marked both by fierce, avoidable sun but also balmy and long-lasting cold, to one of perpetual summer? Why, Mr Tapley, is the lion drawn to the waterhole, or the bat to the exposed rump of a steer in plain sight?

'A rich seam!

'And so, I said to myself, I must simply apply skills of mind honed over decades to the small problem of logic at hand. Looking around Los Angeles, reading the newspapers and company bulletins, waiting patiently in the dying moments of the day for important oil analysts to grace me with their attention, I realised the land was rich indeed – positively spattered with opportunity – and the syndicates which were speculating upon it lay thick as fruit dropping to the ground in autumn. When I wish, I can be extraordinarily persuasive. This again was not the problem. But I wished to engage, to work, and how might that be accomplished when I also needed to live? As dusk fell each day in the mansion, I worked away at my problem. But it was not until a servant, fixing up gutters in the daytime, inadvertently revealed something to me that the solution was revealed.

'"Do you wish to go for dinner?" the man said to his helper, a scrawny young stripling barely rid of his acne. It was this, or some such similar phrase.

'"I do not wish," his companion replied. "I am not hungry now. I prefer to do it later, when the wild things eat. Get me a booth at Cole's, one of them wet sandwiches and some few drinks. That is the ticket."

'It was, indeed, the ticket! For like you, and your helpful waitress with the wily uncle and his skin condition, I too eat as the wild things do. Such establishments exist for eating, so why not for working, also? Was not the business of oil a twenty four hour business, after all? Where the sumps were sunk, the pumps pumping, work did not cease till the earth had belched up its last barrel. So! My direction was set. I needed a syndicate with an all-consuming lust for black gold – a lust so deep-set, so bred into its soul that nothing would sate it once the tap was made, and the spigot drinking its fill. Like *you*, Mr Tapley! A maker of rods and straws and suction devices. This I sought, on the grandest scale! In the usual ways of man, it did not take long.

'The analyst was a broker of sorts, or so he sold himself. A small man with a rather large appetite for money. Henshaw was his name. A fifty dollar bill to his secretary bought me an audience at sunset.

'"Henry Henshaw,' he said, ushering me in. 'Hank. Mr – uh, Carpathian? Marvin Carpathian?'

'"Indeed."

'"So nice to make your acquaintance. Now what can I do for you, this fine day? Or should I say, this lovely evening!"

'"I wish to buy into an oil syndicate. More specifically, I wish to buy in on very advantageous terms to the current owners, so I might work in my own way and using my own powers to enhance the profitability of the business."

'"Terms, you say?" The little man actually licked his chops, like a hyena coming late to the carcass. "You bring any special – uh, talents, to this deal? You an engineer by trade?"

'"No."

'"Got any industry experience, maybe over there in Europe, or wherever?"

"No."

'He smiled a small, strained smile.

'"You ain't making it easy, Marvin, I gotta tell you that. What *do* you bring?"

'I hefted the fat pigskin suitcase at my feet onto his glass desk. Its Bakelite knobs scraped the surface with tiny screeches.

'"These are my terms."

'I flipped the latch, turned the case around so its interior – stuffed with thousands of hundred dollar bills, packed tightly inside one another as in your multi-bird roast – and watched as the wheels went around in his head. He could barely keep from grinning. Henshaw reached out one trembling finger and poked at the suitcase. It did not move. He gripped the edge of the glass, tried with the side of his fist. It landed with a smack beside the clasp, but nothing shifted. The man began to sweat.

'"So this –" he began.

'"I am a very persuasive man, Mr Henshaw. I believe I can bring great value to any syndicate which can accommodate my wishes."

'"And what might those be?"

'"I wish to work at night, to have open access to the books, and to the personnel files of each employee."

'"Personnel?"

'"Yes. That is all."

'After a second of puzzlement he reached out his arms to embrace the suitcase, snapped the clasp and, not without effort, grunted it down to the floor. He pressed a buzzer on the intercom.

'"Florence? Get in here, girl, and pick something up."

'When the secretary had dragged the case out of his office, casting a sideways eye upon my person as she did so, Henshaw sat up crisply in his seat and held out a hand.

'"Mr Carpathian," he said, "let's make this happen."

*

Looking back, I gotta couple observations. First, I don't doubt him – or Henshaw, come to that. Carpathian coulda sold ice to the Eskimoes. He was looking away now, so I had a few moments to myself. I angled the notepad up into the firelight – funny, but I didn't notice before; it was roaring like a hurricane blowing through the whole time, but no one tended the thing, and I couldn't see logs or whatever you'd need to feed a blaze like that – so I could take a gander over what I'd put down. My hand was cramping, each finger thick and unhappy and fused to the next like it was welded together. Still – everything was there. I flipped back over dozens of pages. I'd even gotten the dialogue, though God knew how the guy remembered that.

Second, he was being pretty open – I thought I knew what I was dealing with, crazy as it sounds, and it had little to do with fetes or kewpie dolls – but only in a strict verbal sense. I mean, the guy was gushing, in that refined European way of his. Detail this and detail that; nothing, or so it seemed, was being left out. Sealed, the crate was – yes sir! But not tight enough to prevent a little light snacking.

But here he was – here *it* was – and while I was looking down at my pad, one set of crunched fingers trying to rub the numb out of the ball of my other thumb, warm up those banana-boys for the task to come, suddenly the heavy shadow of his presence was gone. I looked up. He had left chair, and hearth, for a position at the window, arms folded at his sides, face elevated so his eyes matched the slim spaces between the slats.

'Are you well, Mr Tapley?'

At his voice the fire gave another flare. The resulting roar tinkled the glassware on the mantelpiece.

'I – well, yeah, sir, Mr Carpathian. Acourse. Ready for round two, if you are.'

'No – I think we shall talk, you and I, for a moment.'

'Uh – yeah, okay. If that's what you want.'

'It is, indeed, what I want.'

He slipped back into the high-backed chair like a bat returning to roost, and I felt the shadows of the room lengthening, drawing me in. What else did he have to tell me? What else *was* there?

For the moment, he said nothing. I took the chance to study that long saturnine face; fingers arched once more, nails interlocked and sharp as the raw ends of broken timber; even the fine, precise cut of his suit. He wore a black tie, I noticed, or perhaps just maroon darkened by flickering shadows. On one finger a lozenge-shaped ruby. The buttons on his waistcoat glittered like chips of onyx. What was I doing here, really? Taking down this creature's thoughts, but to what end? A wind of fear blew up the nape of my neck, cold fingers bristling my scalp. He had been gazing into the flames, but now turned his eyes back on me.

'I suppose,' Carpathian said, 'you are wondering why such a man –' his hands, breaking apart, swept round the room with lofty arrogance, 'should require the services of a cheap two-bit scribbler in the first place?'

A nasty smile, cold as a toad's back, played across his features.

'Immortality, perhaps? To record my epic deeds in salacious detail, as the reputed chronicler of the old gunslingers in the west did, some decades ago? To inspire fear and awe in those drawn to tales of the tawdrier forms of life?'

His smile disappeared, aided by the dart of a serpentine tongue. I couldn't help myself. It was worth this flogging if I could just keep my hand still, ring up these visual gems in the cash-register. A second, haunted suggestion of amusement crossed his face, brief as the calm in the hollow of a tornado, then was gone. In his eyes now was black and piercing intent.

'I jest, of course, Mr Tapley. Your services are invaluable to me. You may resume taking notes, for memory is fallible, is it not? What takes place in conversations – sparkling as it may be – can often not be reproduced upon the page.'

I flipped a page, cracked my knuckles loudly.

'So what *do* you want me to do for you, with this – uh, this narrative, sir? I can take it two ways, I feel. Play up the horrors and the crimes and the dark rivers of blood – all that. Pulp it up, you know. *Saucy Secrets* the hell out of it. Or I can go the other way. Serious, proper, journalistic. Just the facts, Jack, and let the chips fall where they may.'

'Do you believe I wish to become a cheap dime-store horror, then? A man of my lineage?'

'No – *no!* Of course not. But –'

'Then you have your answer.'

I noticed a grey soupy line had crept between the slats of the blinds, but he waved a hand, dragging my fingers back to the page. It sat, thirsty again, gulch-dry, under the hot ball of my thumb. I set out to water it, and was swallowed up whole by a canyon.

*

'You will remember nothing of this period of time, beyond that which I permit. Your eyes are tied to my finger, my voice, with the tightest of cords. Any thought which occurs to you has passed first from me, and all words on the page beneath your finger belong to me – are in my service – and you are nothing at all. Close your eyes. Your fingers will work of their own accord, at my direction alone. Relax into your chair as though your body had no weight. Lie back. Lie back, Raymond. Good. Your hand is a float, tethered to a distant line, and bobbing upon the waters of my voice. Your will is submerged. I pull on the string, you respond in kind, and we begin.

'I have no desire to tell my own legend, with embellishments or curlicues, as those gunslingers hand-tooled their holsters, or etched filigrees into the barrels of their guns. Quite the opposite. I wish you to take all of your powers – the raw splendour of Miss McTavish, the blood and sweat of her conquests, even the small clunking tales of suburban life with its petty disputes and picayune victories – and turn them inside out. I wish no show to be made of my deeds. Meals served in a slab are no gourmet repast, but sliced to slivers of delight, tickle the palate, and further the enlightenment of the reader.

'This is what I wish: that the world knows of my kind, our means of survival, in its raw and unadorned state. I take no pleasure from it. I am no longer sure I ever did. Your chilling romance writers, Mr Tapley, portray such things as great and glorious shockers – the dark room, draped in shadow and cobweb, corners looming round a fragile yet beautiful heroine, her skin chalk white, white as a blank page upon which the claret will shortly pour. Further gothic elements are added: crumbling stone, ivy, an inward-swinging gate of immense size, sure to produce the requisite groan, which in turn will echo around a high space lit only by a flickering lamp. You may add a bat or two, if you wish.

'Into this preposterous scenario, the monster comes. Stark chords of an organ, Mr Tapley, shrieking strings. The maiden raises one trembling hand to her cheek. And I strike! Yet the reality is much sadder and more drab than such fantasies.

'In my home, I live alone, it is true. A large house, but not an opulent one; my ancestors ruled, but the land was bitter, and more could not be wrung from it than it would give. A woman comes now and again to rag and mop the place when I am away, crossing herself and throwing sheets over my mirrors, I believe. I do not care. I shall never see the house again.

'I wake, and sometimes I am hungry. There is no music to accompany the creaking of the bed as my weight unwinds its hinges. It is dark and cold and I go to my food. The village is not like your great and teeming Los Angeles. The sun, had I a wish to see it, barely penetrates the cloud which swirls constantly about the mountain. The peasants are wrapped tight in their dirty rags against the cold. Here is need, desperation and fury. Such things season the meat, but cannot satisfy. I do not dress impeccably, as your screen monsters do, to roam the village and environs. A coarse black jacket, shoes with thick soles ribbed for sucking mud. I pass behind the outhouses and under the low veranda of the common hall, where gas lamps' feeble fingers cannot probe. I peel open my collar against the possibility of a meal.

'There is no glamour, Mr Tapley. There is no longer even terror. When I come upon an old woman, a small child – for I wish no struggles – the light of life dies suddenly in their eyes as I take sustenance. I do not abandon them on the path, for it is a small place; I lay them beneath the graveyard wall for their relatives to find. Life in the mountains is short and hard. When I return, I leave the house for a few months to wander at dusk, then find sanctuary in some other crumbling mansion which I have not visited in its turn for many years. There is no glamour in any of it.

'I see your fingers pause. Cease to think. Merely obey. Your talent is useful to me only as I direct it. There is no glamour, Mr Tapley, but there is learning. On the mountain, the nights are long, but tallow is cheap. I read of this great country from papers and magazines – tattered, yes, and tired from their journey – and later saw juddering soundless films of her plains and skyscrapers, docks as wide as the world. In those faces I saw, and imagined, hungers such as I endured, but magnified a thousandfold – lust for food, excitement, possessions; greed for money that oiled the wheels of longing; desire to touch the golden creatures who strode down avenues of light.

'So when I came, all seemed natural; peaceful, the end point of some hidden destiny, some working-out of all to the good. But when bodies began to drop about the harbour – the railroad yard, the sidings, the alleyways behind great boulevards and the hidden hollows of your gentle hills, then came the usual screaming.

'Why, Mr Tapley?

'Do you not recognise that you and I – all these tanned, happy natives of the golden shore – 'are in essence the same?'

'This is unfair, is it not? I thirst but can never quench. Your kind burns the ancient wick of the world, and can never drink enough. So: the Syndicate stands, I work well and hard – though some say at odd hours, it is true – and where your engines seek nourishment, I provide it, at a most handsome return. All is well with the world.'

*

Carpathian snapped his fingers, and my pen stopped mid-word. A sudden ringing sprang up in my ears, keen as a moistened thumb around a glass, then was gone. The fire too died away. Dawn, it seemed, was coming. I looked up.

'Everything you've said, Mr Carpathian – Marvin – I understand, I truly do. I get it. Life's hard. Things are difficult, even for a successful guy like you. But I don't see – '

His gaze snapped into mine, locking in with the precise click of a door latch.

'What do you not see?'

'Well, I just – see, ya know – well, Marvin – Mr Carpathian, sir – ya gotta understand, it's a helluva hard sell.'

He smiled, then laughed. In the cavernous dark of his mouth silver sparks jumped about like fleas. He flexed his fingers and all the bones in his knuckles popped, one by one, with the percussive racket of a Chinatown sidewalk.

'Of course. That is why I brought you here. Do you not see?'

And the odd thing was, I did. I looked at him in the pale, flabby light of dawn – he'd withdrawn slightly into the protective shadow of his chair – in his sharp-cut suit and dark, slick hair, the last of the dying firelight running down the razor blades of his cheekbones, and I got it. It was the hardest sell in the world.

I looked from vampire to oil executive, and from oil executive to vampire, then from vampire to oil executive again; but already it was impossible to say which was which. I shrugged, flexed my swollen fingers, and got down to it.

Monica would understand.

I often did my best work in the evenings.

The New New Colossus, or All Aboard!

1

'IT'S PRONOUNCED *PRATTLE*, by God! How many times do I have to tell you people?'

The newshound looked on impassively, rolling a damp cheroot from one side of his mouth to the other. He checked Stella's cheat-sheet (again) for this contract duo's stage name: Globe & Pratfall. Or *Prattle*, he supposed. McIntyre sighed round the end of his cigar.

'Now you've got me started,' the lanky one continued – the other sat silent as a fireplug, beefy hands locked around a cup of coffee – 'an while it's true he does look a mite portly – alright, a bit more than a mite – so that his name seems to fit, it ain't nothing whatsoever to do with that. It's a fine old Scottish moniker, see, what his people brought over from the glens and mountains and that there. *Globe*, ya know. Look it up.'

There was a momentary, welcome interruption, then another voice intruded.

'Shove over sideways, Mac. Need a better angle. Yeah, that's it.'

The newshound's sidekick leant over for a better shot, flash-bulb poised, the arm of his camera reaching in like a metal finger and dimpling his colleague's hat.

'Davis – hey! Tryin to work, here.'

'Sorry, Mac. All done.' He nodded and grinned. 'See ya back at the roost.'

McIntyre fiddled for a minute, taking off his hat and fingering it into shape, before getting comfortable again on his side of the booth. The skinny one – Prattle, by God – was still leaning out into no man's land, fingers waving around like some undersea beast feeling the way out of its lair. The fat one remained inert, jammed up against the mirror at the far end, hands bound everlastingly to cup. His fingers, thick as sausages, bristled with dense black hair that crawled up and over his knuckles. More than he had left up top, the journalist noted, sourly. What a pair. One high falutin streak-of-piss, running over at the mouth, and his husky, silent pal.

Still, *something* was keeping him here, beyond his editor's deadline. Most likely the looks he'd get from Stella, who'd booked this thing in for her *Movie Madness* slot, and wouldn't take kindly to having to write up some other bit of fluff at this late stage. He sighed again, manoeuvring his smoke into the business position. Flipping his notebook open to a virgin page, he tipped his hat and cracked a phoney smile.

'So, fellas,' he said. 'Globe & Pratfall. What's that all about?'

2

'And? What did you think?'

'About what?'

'Those two movie *klowns*, you *klutz* – what the hell else?'

They were in bed, after hours, the copy put to bed and nothing on but a lamp in the corner. Stella's shoulders poked from under the coverlet. She'd done her nails, and one set of pink piggies was gently taking the air. McIntyre tugged at his undershirt. The damn thing was damp, with no pocket, and he had no place to lodge his stogie. How come she always looked so cool? For that matter, how did she always plough through his prose and make it come out snappier every time?

'Well, if you must know, I thought they were hiding something. Maybe several somethings, under all that yak and silence. Like some secret, some *revelation.*' He accented the last word so she would see it in sixty point type.

'Oh – do tell! Why wasn't this in the piece?'

He reached down to pull on a sparkling toenail, but the piggy retreated to safety. McIntyre put light to another.

'Are you saying my piece blew, Stella, that it? You coulda done the damn thing yourself, and saved me the bother.'

'Now, Mac, who's being a baby, and who's really interested, like a professional? I didn't say it blew – it *was* a bit soft here and there, sure, but what isn't? I got the magic pencil, after all – but hell, now you've got me really interested. What did you mean?'

'I don't know.'

He waited for a moment to see if the pout might pay dividends, but nothing doing.

'Well, take the two of them. All at odds physically, like that other pair – you know, limey and fat boy. Whatsisname, Georgia.'

'Yeah, I know.'

She smiled her editor's flat, indulgent smile.

'So one's tall and rangy, right, like an electric string-bean, and the other's sorta squat and hairy, like something straight outta the woods. Not just physically, either; personally too. The big lunk never said word one, just sat there nipping at his coffee now and then, watching the shadows lengthen in the mirror. The other one talked like a happy-dust freak, hands all over the place, going at it lickety-split and never shutting up. I barely got a word in edge-wise.'

'So?'

'What d'ya mean, so?'

'I mean so far, so what. They're a couple of oddballs. Gimme the *juice*. What were they hiding?'

'Well,' he said again, leaning back and taking a long contemplative drag. 'That's the question now, isn't it? Grant the fact they knew I was a reporter, and that what reporters do – depending on how friendly they are, with yours truly the friendliest, most sincerest hound in the pack, you understand – is to pick up on the interesting stuff they're trying to hide away, blow up the pre-packaged crap and see what surfaces. I don't know, though. I can't quite put my finger on it. They didn't play the game, is what I *do* know.'

She raised an eyebrow and reached for his smoke.

'Unseemly.'

'Blow it out your ass. So what you're saying is, they didn't yield to your charms, right? Didn't melt like a pat of butter under the hot, thrusting knife of interrogation?'

'Now you're just being unnecessary. Wrong, too. They did the usual – dance round the soft spots, fence the hard questions, wedge in all that tired hoo-ha about art. But the one I couldn't shut up, and the other might as well've been dead for all the juice I got out of him.'

'So maybe they aren't that interesting. Take the other pair. Fatboy likes the ladies, I've heard, and the limey's never off set. Always tinkering around, never satisfied, while his buddy's forever itching for the links. Maybe you should go talk to them instead.'

McIntyre remained still. In the quiet they heard the crackle of his tobacco touch a knuckle, the mad honk of passing automobiles.

'No,' he said, 'I think I'll stick with them. Find out what makes them tick. Might even go for a feature.'

She raised an eyebrow and in a feat of limber athleticism, poked her piggies up under his vest. They said no more about it.

3

'Newsroom.'

He picked up the receiver with one hand while the other kept on pecking at the keys. He was expecting to hear from Ivy Close, an English starlet he'd interviewed Monday for a mini-feature on the international draw of Hollywood. She was from Stockton, she'd said, giggling, only not the one he was familiar with. As he put the phone to his ear, he was sure he was about to hear all the glories of some piddling little English burg, so splendid and charming he simply *must* hop a steamer and see it for himself. But instead a man's voice, gruff and resonant, came bowling down the line.

'Hello? I was trying to reach Mr McIntyre.'

'This is McIntyre. How can I help you?'

He sat up and yanked his tie straight, running a hand through his mop and trying to put a little authority into his voice. This guy sounded like business.

'Ah, Mr McIntyre – yes. Thank you so much for taking my call. This is Alvin Bugge, at the studio.'

He didn't need the name.

'Yes, Mr Bugge! Hello. Yes, sir. How can I be of assistance?'

There was the clump of a desktop humidor, and after a significant moment, the snick of a lighter.

'I believe you've written a short – ah, piece – on two of my contract players. I've read it, of course; I like to keep up to date with all my people, and I do *so* admire your style.

'Furthermore, your editor mentioned you intend to pursue a longer series on them, their work as well as the usual personality material. Is that correct?'

Was this guy in bed last night? He briefly pictured smacking each little piggy with a boot-heel, till they gave up the ghost.

'Ah, yes, Mr Bugge, that's right. My editor has approved a series on Globe & Pratfall. A fascinating act, I must say, and thank you for the compliment.'

'Think nothing of it, Mr McIntyre. It's no more than the truth.'

'So, yes. A feature, over a few editions possibly. Did my editor outline the general feel of the thing?'

'Admirably.'

'Then – ah, how might I help?'

'A very good question.' McIntyre thought he heard the man run a hand down his vest, the crackle of expensive cloth readjusting itself. Perhaps he was cracking up. 'Those fellows are indeed rather interesting. A profitable investment for the studio, I should say, at least in the long-term. A definite investment in art right away. Yet I have – what should I say? A trifling reservation.'

'Oh – of what sort?'

'The sort that costs money, Mr McIntyre. In my business, the worst possible kind. Ambition, in short. Now you have met them, I should be very grateful if you could bear in mind that the talkative partner – Mr, ah, Pratfall – can occasionally overreach himself, and the *silent* partner, Mr Globe, often fails to restrain his colleague's vaulting enthusiasms.'

'Does this have anything to do with my feature?'

'Oh, no! And yet, perhaps so. I was merely calling to afford you a little inside knowledge of the pair, and advise, perhaps caution, you to temper Mr Pratfall's wilder speculations with a dose of journalistic sangfroid.'

'Not a problem, sir; no problem at all. Thank you for the tip-off.'

Bugge drew in smoke for a moment longer, and the line cleared. McIntyre leant back in his chair, then snapped to all of a sudden and stuffed a fresh sheet of paper into the machine. He had just begun typing when the phone rang again. He loosened his tie, picked up.

'Ivy! How lovely to hear from you – '

4

A few days later, and surprisingly early – Stella had warned him to ditch his preconceptions about movie people – he found himself on a sound stage, or a set or whatever they called the damn thing, working a tall paper cup of coffee and a crippling hangover. They'd had it out the day before, over Bugge and her indiscretions. For once they hadn't tumbled into bed at the end but parted with a round of curt remarks, and no worries at all about letting the sun go down on their anger. He'd headed back to his apartment with a fifth and an ice-pick. He wasn't sure where she had ended up, and at this point, didn't care.

'Just make sure you get the good stuff,' she said before he slammed out. 'I gotta bunch of slots to fill, and audiences can't seem to get enough of these duos, even the lame ones. The *good* stuff, Mac.' Even angry, up on her high-horse, she was still fetching, damn her.

He dabbed at his throbbing forehead with a handkerchief. Perhaps a little lean on this two-by-four might settle things down. The wood was stiff but sort of slippery-cool, and reclining he laid his neck against a fat wedge of plaster.

'Hey, buddy!'

An insistent Asian man was suddenly barking in his ear. He wore a white cap, a tight golfing shirt. The muscles flexed in his forearms as he moved.

McIntyre's brow creased again.

'Wh – what, now?'

'Move yer ass, if you please – sideways, backways, don't care. Gotta get the shot set up and that don't include you.'

McIntyre groaned, unpeeling himself from the scenery, and staggered away into the dark. It was some *trompe-l'oeil* sort of thing, he noticed, as the man wheeled it by; lumpen and crude sailing past your face, but ever more elegant as it receded. An arched doorway, with a hint beyond of a room down a short hall, some kind of painted sunlight spilling onto wood. He liked it, but it wasn't around long enough to really admire. The technician bumped past and steered it round a corner, a slight smile on his face.

McIntyre sat down on the rim of a barrel, his ass numb but grateful for the perch. In the dimness he closed his eyes and let the coffee do its work. Maybe some of that old movie magic would rub off and he'd wake up someplace else, on another day, with the damn feature written and Stella finally off his back. He smiled, but it didn't last.

A moment later a series of high, sharp cracks rang around the place and the biggest lights he'd ever seen came on overhead, to the sides, and right in front of him; in rumpled suit and dented hat, he felt like a waterbug wandering across a wedding-cake. He stood up, aligning the visitor pass with his tie-clip (why did he bother?) and buffing the tops of his shoes on the relatively clean cloth of each calf.

After a minute McIntyre looked around and realised no one was watching him, or cared a fig about how he looked. No one, indeed, seemed to know he was there. He looked at his watch – yes, ten on the dot, just like Pratfall said; in fact quarter after – and Pratfall was nowhere to be seen, with Globe absent, too. About a thousand technical types dashed about, adjusting the artificial world till its crooked edges aligned, the flat patches of colour and splashes of light were set at their correct angles. He walked head-on towards the open door, dumping his cup and looking round in wonder.

Behind him, smells of dust and plaster lingered. He barely heard the thousand footsteps, rattling castors and squeaking joints as the set guys levered everything into place. He walked open-mouthed into a country house, and smiled. McIntyre could almost smell the polish wafting up from the wooden floor. Somewhere, no doubt, a lithe and spirited young woman was reclining on a couch, raising one decorous arm, perhaps yawning like a cat. A butler was off stage polishing the silver, and the whole scene waited on someone's pleasure. Whose might that be? Why *his*, of course! He smiled like an idiot and padded over to the door.

'Hey!'

The same technician appeared and grabbed his elbow, ramming him off set.

'Thanks, Mac. Out with you. And *stay* out.'

The man pointed to a door – this one real, dinged with nicks and scratches like a gangster's forearms – before propelling McIntyre through it with one unyielding shove. 'Have a nice day, now.'

On the other side the world was calm, dull and dim. He looked around him, and what he'd assumed must be a back way out of the warehouse, even off the lot, was in fact another connected room, this one tall and skinny with a barren, neglected look. As his eyes adjusted he saw Globe and Pratfall balancing like mannequins on the top and bottom of an enormous spiral staircase.

'Boys,' said McIntyre, falling gracelessly into a canvas chair. 'You mind?'

He did not, in fact, care. The canvas was baggy and moulded itself to his skinny shoulders like a grandmother's embrace. 'Never mind.'

He wasn't sure they heard him, and was happy enough to sit, though missed the blinding celestial vision of the country house in this shabby annexe. The two of them remained still, poised between railings, Globe on a squat metal platform at the foot, Pratfall at the top, his arms draped through twisted *fleur-de-lys* iron shapes. As he peered, he could see they were in fact moving; not quickly, or decisively, but with a stealthy persistence, from angle to angle around the stair, pushing at the metal, testing its give.

Suddenly Globe sprang to his feet and jumped, once, in place. The platform gave a satisfying bong, but didn't move. Pratfall waited a beat, then extracting his arms from the metalwork, jumped in similar fashion, as though a wave of unstoppable motion had finally reached him.

'Good?' Globe said. His voice was low and rough, more a grunt than anything else, a hound-dog patted for picking up the trail.

'Yep.'

Pratfall's he knew, though this curt version was something of a revelation. The man was intent, waiting like a pond-skater for all the ripples in the surface tension to reach him, then stroked the handrail and bounced down to ground level.

'Mr McIntyre,' he said with a half-sneer. 'Gracing us with your presence?'

'Well – ah, yeah, you know. This *is* the time, right? Where we agreed to meet, and all?'

Globe nodded but contributed nothing further. He set off round the back of the staircase, whose fastenings he now appeared to be loosening from the earth – great bolts clanging up into the platform, the sound huge, piercing – and when he was finished, pulled its entire fifteen-foot span around in a circle, pushing it towards the back of the room.

'Sure is, bub. Still interested?'

McIntyre had just watched a man disassemble one significant aspect of a country pile, ordinarily fixed and unmoving, before shooing it from the room like a reluctant pooch. How could he not be?

5

'We're done here for now. Let's get a cup.'

'And – Globe?'

'Don't worry bout him. He's got shit to be gettin on with. Follow me.'

They walked into deeper gloom at the back of the space, where Globe had disappeared with his machine, and an enormous hinged door appeared. Pratfall moved to the right, pushing at a smaller man-sized cut out, and they were back in the hanger-like studio. Globe was nowhere to be seen, but the staircase had already migrated into place, bridging the two stories of the country house. Pratfall nodded.

'Later.'

They came to a side-door, which he rather curiously held open like a suitor for his lady, then they were out in the glaring sun.

'Goddamn furnace.'

Pratfall took out a pair of flat black sun-glasses, tucked his head into his chest. 'Come on, bub, before we get roasted. Lightin film's the only thing it's good for.'

McIntyre's head began to spin with the heat and heady mix of contrary impressions. The morning was not turning out as he had expected, yet he still had little for the notebook, and Stella – blast her eyes – would be waiting when he finally crawled back to his apartment. She wouldn't have her hand out; wouldn't need to.

'Hey, Pratfall – hold up.'

The taller half of the duo was already fifty yards away, barrelling like a horny rooster for the dark of the chicken-coop. He didn't look up, and McIntyre had to scuttle just to catch him. Around a giant pair of scaly legs, seemingly abandoned in front of a wall painted like a blue sky, then a handcart stacked with boxes of dusty boots, and Pratfall was gone again. A swing door was whooshing closed, and McIntyre caught it just before the rubber seals clapped shut. He went into the cool. A whistle from the back and he saw his man, hat in hand and glasses off, ordering at a zinc bar on the far side of the room. McIntyre walked over slowly and fell into a chair.

'Coffee?'

Sure – who cared? His head was a little better, but his eyes felt like the last few pithy strands of orange peel caught on the rim of a trashcan. He closed them again. As he lay back in the arch of the seat, his notebook jutted from his pocket. Who cared about that, either. At least the light in here was soft. He supposed he'd have to try and make the best of it.

A few minutes later, Pratfall sat down opposite.

'There y'are, boy. Coffee. What am I supposed to call ya, anyways? I already got through bub and feller, but you must hava handle you prefer,'

'Mac. Mac's fine, Mr Pratfall.'

'Aw never mind all that stage-show shit. Get it right in the articles, mind you, don't get me wrong, but call me Gene.'

'Gene, then. Gene it is.'

'Mac.'

'Gene.'

They both smiled.

'You wanna know why I got you away from all that there – sets, lights an everything?'

'Globe – what's his name, if you don't mind my asking?'

'He's Globe. Don't you wonder, though, Mac? I mean, I read your gal's fluff pieces like everyone else in the trade, an I'm glad she's pullin in the payin folk, know what I mean? But she don't exactly seem fond of the *trade* itself. More personalities, money an all that shit. I thought you and I could jaw bout something a bit more interestin.'

'Well, she's not exactly my gal, but okay.'

'You don't say? Seemed pretty chummy on the old 'phone, to me.'

He raised one eyebrow and flashed a quick comic wiggle through the wrinkles on his forehead. Mac could see the appeal, and wondered if he'd spent time in Vaudeville before heading west. With that face, he could easily hold an audience captive in the gods.

'So what's the deal with you and Mr – ah, with you and Globe? You said back in the diner he doesn't like to talk, prefers to get on with the business. You, however, seem like a champion talker to me. Why the double act?'

Gene leaned back in his chair, his long body arching over the rounded aluminium, arms stretching out wide, then snapped back straight and took up his coffee.

'That, sir, demands a long answer, and one I can't entirely give – not today, anyways.' He gestured with the rim of his cup towards the dormant notebook, and McIntyre uncapped his pen. 'For the record, see, Globe is a genius. No two ways about it. The things he can do with his hands, his face, his body, on film, off it, on stage, wherever. No one can touch him. I'm just riding his coat-tails. But he don't like to talk about nothin at all, and that's fine with me.'

'What do you mean, things? Like what?'

Gene sipped, curling his hands tightly round the porcelain (a bit like his partner, McIntyre observed).

'Take this staircase, here. Country house, right? Nice place. You saw the illusion. Dame's in the parlour, all dolled up, drinking hot tea and whatnot outta them little fancy cups, butler's polishin the silver, the whole nine yards. Not sure where the man of the house is, quite yet, but the gag boys're workin on it. Anyways, this is a short, right? Not a feature, nothing too fancy, but Bugge wants his money's worth and figures the bigger the better, if it's a hit it might make a series, even a full picture. I think he fancies himself a bit of a lord, you know, but he ain't too high and mighty to take a few pot-shots at them people. So Globe an me, we're outta the writin loop – them boys keep themselves to themselves; we're lucky if we see the script the day before we shoot – but Bugge puts round this memo statin how, in his humble opinion, the picture should be both 'humorous and affectionate', whatever the hell that means. Like, are we sendin up these posh clowns, or not? So in this scenario me and Globe's the handymen trying to fix things up some in the old pile, maybe before the man of the house comes back from the war, or some shit. I don't know.'

All very interesting, Mac thought. The guy had a way with words his partner was sorely lacking. But what was so special about it, after all that?

'So we're hangin round while they're changing the lights for the early stuff, see – wifey all broken up but not showing nothin in front of the butler – and we hear these two gag-boys chewin over how can they make somethin funny without being cruel to the nobs, ya know. Like the funnin comes outta the hurtin, right? And Globe, he pulls me aside, says, "Gene, I gottan ideer for dis, no problem." An I says, "Ideer? What sorta ideer?" An he says, "A good wun, see. I know it'll work. If I get it it up and runnin, will you talk to them boys?" An I says,

"You know I will, bub, you *know* I will." So he nods and smiles, sorta low, like, and off he goes. We was finishin up this morning when you come in.'

Mac took a long drink of his cooling brew, still none the wiser.

'And?'

'Whatta ya mean, and? Ain't it obvious?'

McIntyre held up his notebook, a big curly question mark doodled over the page.

'Humour me.'

Pratfall sighed. He drained his cup and pushed it aside, stretched out his arms as though he was going to pump someone's hand, or maybe pick up a baby for a politician to kiss. He grew still and his eyes burned into McIntyre's.

'I'd tear you one off right now, Mac, if I thought you was tryin it on, but I don't. I figure Mr Sourmash is still in charge, and that's alright, but listen up – brush away them cobwebs, now. I only needed to hear this once and I knew it would work, and I *also* knew I couldn't never have thought of it in a million years. Globe, though – well, I don't know if what he does is thinkin or just doin. But it took him maybe two minutes to sell me on it – that, and a few other things.'

Gene arched his eyebrow.

'So, the staircase. What, you may say, is so damn special about it? Well think about what it does. The thing winds up, bottom to top, and sorta conveys whoever's on it from one state to another, right? First floor to second, downstairs to upstairs. Nothing to it, right? Wrong. That's Globe's genius right there. It don't just convey somebody somewheres, it kinda transports 'em, ya know – the lady, goin upstairs, to get a view down the drive where hubby maybe's on his way; she feels hopeful, now. The butler, he spends his time with the motley crew downstairs, right, walks up her ladyship's morning tray, he's going up in the world, even for a minute. Well what if we come in to fix this shuggly thing – steps is broke, maybe, railings out, or some other shit (it don't matter) and now we're loopin and swayin and wobblin round in place, but can't get up, down or nothing else – then the lady she sees it and feels better, and the butler sees it and maybe takes some funnies out, too. That way we ain't rippin on the nobs or the peasants, but givin em both something to laugh at. It's like healing, Globe says. The thing's hinged in the middle and he and I are goin ta hang on for dear life while it swings around the set with our balls in the wind. *That's* what I mean about Globe. Them gag boys took about a second to get on board, and we're shootin it this afternoon.'

As Gene talked, McIntyre's thumping head began to recede. He could see the clean space of the country pile's hallway, door standing inwards, the lady somewhere behind it, perhaps the butler's shadow breaking into the bars of sun on the floor. Then through that calm, sad space come these two lunatic clowns – one cranky, pop-eyed and garrulous, the other a silent fireplug – both revolving in mid-air, like a flying dame in a puffy skirt, a pug-dog suspended on a high wire. It could work.

'I get it,' he said. 'I think I do. How long did Globe take to come up with this?'

'Who knows, Mac. Ain't no tellin. But no time at all as far as I could tell.'

They sat for a minute in the cool of the metal fans, chewing it over. With the coffee and mental gymnastics, his lizard-brain had finally crawled out onto the rock, and was basking in the warm sun of an idea.

'I don't suppose – well, no, not really.'

'What?'

'I just – sort of thought, it might be interesting – for the article, the series, you know – might be fascinating, even, to see that in action.'

'See what?'

'The Globe thing. You, too, of course. What makes the pair of you tick.'

'Beyond the money – *hah!* – and all the fine dames, you mean?'

'Yes, beyond those things.'

Pratfall scratched his chin, gave great attention to the impression he was thinking things over.

'I'd need to talk to Globe, ya know.'

'Of course.'

'An he'd get a veto. No yay, no go. Can't get round it. Not wi Globe.'

'Not a problem. I can swing it with Stella on my end.'

They looked at each other for a moment, then smiled and shook hands. McIntyre rubbed his forehead and closed the flap on his notebook, then reconsidered and tore out the top page, crumpled it into a ball and dropped it in the dregs of his coffee. She'd have to drag it out of him with chains. She'd have to beg, grovel and plead for something this good, and to hell with little lapses in faith, or lost confidences. She'd have to come to him.

Mac nodded once more, and smiled.

6

It was definitely the desert.

'It's desert, Mac,' Stella said, shuffling across the bench to the far window and extending an arm beyond the side mirror. 'Look – cactuses, scrubby ball-weed things. Little outcrops of rock, but mostly nothing.'

While she waved her arm about, cigarette trailing smoke in its wake, he fumed. He knew it was the desert – the Mojave, to be precise, and he knew that she knew he knew that it was – but here he was again taking all of her crap for the good of a story. She did look good wearing that sheath dress, mind you, and her new wavy do was rather fetching in the slow-rolling billows of wind coming in the window. But dammit – he hadn't intended for her to accept when he told her about Pratfall's invitation; quite the opposite. He'd undersold the thing as a dreary chore, a trip to some godforsaken hell-hole in the back of beyond, all dust and lizards and ladders in her stockings, but she had to find a sense of adventure.

'Yes, Stella, I know that. Didn't I say it might get a bit wild. His words, by the way, not mine. Pull your arm in a minute.'

'What?'

'In – yank it in, back inside.'

She did as he asked, and he leaned up near the steering wheel to have a gander at the car trailing along behind. Pratfall's was still in front, keeping up a steady fifty, seemingly unruffled by the heat, but Globe's heap was dwindling to nothing in the mirror. He laid on the horn to get the little caravan's attention.

'Oh Mac, now what?'

'Shaddap, will you Stella? We don't want no one losing anyone, not out here.'

He noticed Pratfall pull over underneath a sagging telephone line – at least they were still within reach of the world – and drew up alongside him. Outside the car, without a breeze slipping in, the air was thick and insufferable. Not like the city, where at least the buildings pulled some wind down between them, if you were lucky, and on still days there were fans and blocks of ice, but wild and untamed, with an electric sizzle and the faint whiff of sour tobacco.

Gene got out of the car and came up to the window.

'Mac? Gotta problem?'

'Globe, I think. His car isn't keeping pace, and I don't want to lose him, not – well, you know. Out here.'

'Goddammit.' Pratfall phlegmmed up a brown mouthful, hawking it high and wide over the roof. Beside him, Stella sniffed. 'Alright, hell – it *is* a piece of shit. Turn round and we'll go pick up that tubby son of a bitch. He'll be burnin up by now.'

When they reached Globe's car he was a sorry sight – stripped half-naked in the sun and trying to tie his waistcoat to a telegraph pole for a skimpy bit of shade. McIntyre pulled up alongside. He was surprised at the man's physique. He looked like a fireplug, sure, and with his shirt off a little like an unhappy black bear scrounging through empty trash cans, but there was no flab to be seen. Flesh lay in great ripples on his barrel-like frame, and the same hair that bristled on his fingers wound around his torso like a black pelt.

Globe nodded, and was about to get in behind Stella when Pratfall pulled up.

'Hey – *hey!*'

He bounded across and snapped the soggy waistcoat off its pole, flicking it at his buddy's backside. In the desert silence the crack echoed for miles. 'Whaddya think *you're* doin? Get up front there, and you – Mac – getcher ass into mine.'

He leaned through the window and Mac recoiled.

'Sorry, bub. Just needta ask the lady here – you okay to drive, miss? Only Globe don't do so good when he's had a skinful of trouble. He probly needs a rest.'

He smiled like a death's head, then withdrew.

'Got stuff to talk about, Mac. He won't bother your lady-friend any.'

He looked back at Stella and she nodded, casting an apprehensive eye sideways as the great bear of a man adjusted his clothes and thudded onto the bench.

'I'll be fine,' she said, ignoring McIntyre and smiling at Globe.

'Nice to finally meet you,' she said. He smiled back.

In Pratfall's car, which had all its windows down and picked up a nice breeze as they pulled away, Mac finally felt himself beginning to relax. He trailed an arm down the side panel, drummed his fingers on its hot metal skin.

'So. What did you want to talk about?'

'Oh, ya know – this and that.'

Gene looked at Globe and Stella a hundred yards back, then out of both windows, peering to the utmost reaches of his side mirrors, making the same circuit again before winding his eyes back in and placing a finger over his lips.

'This,' he said, 'and most *definitely* that.'

7

'*So.* My boy's back there with yer lady, an here we are with an hour or so to go. Ya know, till we get there.'

'Okay. Where is there, exactly?'

'Oh ya know – *there*, where we're goin. The location.'

'Alright. A set, then? Like the staircase, or the country house?'

'Naw, Mac, it's a *location.* I mean there'll be sets there, acourse, once we're up and runnin. But right now it's a location, and a pretty damn fine one at that.'

'A location.'

'Yeah.'

'For a movie.'

'Yeah.'

'And we're going out for a look-see, then, the four of us?'

'Yeah. That's it. A look – he-he-he.'

'I don't like the sound of that, Gene, I've got to say.'

'What! Whadda ya mean?'

'I mean you're sitting there sniggering like a hyena, and your pal back there, old fireplug, he's sitting next to Stella on a sticky car bench with half his clothes missing and his damn jalopy clapped out in the back of beyond. And *I'm* sitting here with you, and you're making all these mysterious noises – that's what I mean.'

'Oh – right.'

'Yeah. So maybe make with something by way of an explanation, seeing as I'm here and all.'

'Alright, Mac. Jeez – ya don't gotta get sore about it. I'll tell ya. Whatta ya wanna know?'

'Well, this movie location: what is it, and come to that, *where* is it?'

'It's out in the desert, see. Beautiful. Not like this old road here, still connected to the city, but really out there. Pure, ya know; desert.'

'And why's that important?'

'Did ya not hear what I said, bub? Didn' ya catch Globe's show?'

'Well – '

'Ah hell, never mind. Now look. This is what you needta know. Movies is about image, right? We've only haddem for about thirty, forty years; before that, you wanted entertainment, some sorta spectacle, you took the wifey down ta Vaudeville or some fancy theatre, ya know, if you was a posh type. That was wings and scenery and ropes an all; basic. Didn't transport you up an away into the sky with somethin huge. That's what movies do – grab ya by the eyeballs, pull ya right outta yer seat.'

'Okay, I get it – the thrill of the show, spectacle, like you say. But what does that have to do with this location?'

'Oh, quite a bit, Mac. You'll see. But lemme tell ya what I wanta tell ya, in the order I wanna do it, okay? So – spectacle, theatre, wings an all that shit, right? It's there, but it's all just *there*, if you know what I mean.'

'There?'

'Yeah – rooted, in the one spot. Kinda stuck. You can't do nothin with it in yer head. But movies, and specially the kind I'm thinkin of, they're in a different league, a different ball game altogether. Hell, the kind me an Globe is plannin, I'm not sure it's even a *game* at all.'

'What's that pole, over there?'

'Eh? Oh, one a the markers – good spot, Mac. Means it's – ah, lemme see now, oh yeah – just unner an hour till we're there. So, anyways, ya with me?'

'Yes – just assume I am, Gene.'

'Well, the big ideer is – sorta, well – the big thing's in Globe's head, but as I get it, the big thing's about what we can show coming right outta the screen, makin its point that way.'

'What point?'

'Well, that some things is bigger than others. That's pretty much it. It's America, ya know.'

'Give me a second. I don't mean to be rude, and I can see you and Globe have got your heads screwed on right, but which things exactly are going to make the point you want to make?'

'Did ya know the first film they ever showed was of a train? Back there in France or England or someplace, with a cloth thrown up on a wall and the projector on a table behind people's heads. Crude, really; nothin to it. But when the lights went down and them beams started flickerin – they'd shot a train, pullin out of some rinky-dink station – there was a riot, see! They'd shot it comin right at the camera, and them folk scrambled up like a packa wild dogs and beat feet for the exit! Thought it was comin right *at* 'em!'

'Is that true?'

'It's the God's honest truth, boy! Pretty much splattered their britches gettin out!'

'Okay – that I can buy. It's a spectacle, alright. Something like that would jump right off the screen and into people's heads.'

'Yeah, yeah. That's it, Mac! Now yer cookin. But think about this. What's the biggest thing people bring to mind when you ask em about America, and I don't mean nona yer skyscrapers and shit. They're outta the way, huge ya know, too big ta fit inside some regular's Joe's noggin.'

'Ah – I dunno, a corn field, maybe? Amber waves, all that?'

'Yeah, maybe, but think bigger, more human.'

'I, ah – hmmm. Well – an ocean liner, maybe, pulling up to the dock?'

'Getting closer! Yer close at that. And what, pray tell, does yer average American, maybe not now but a generation back fer sure, see when he chucks his cardboard case onta the dock?'

'Oh – the Statue of Liberty!'

'You got it, Mac! Lady Liberty herself. Came from France too, if I remember right, just like the movies. She was the biggest thing ever, an right away she got stuck like a burr in people's heads. Can't hardly shake her outta there, even now.'

'So you want to make a movie about the Statue of Liberty?'

'No, Mac! Are you even listenin? Take Lady Liberty and sorta push her over to one sida ya brain. Right, *think* about it – she was the whadda you call it, ya know, for the last century, right?'

'I don't know. Symbol, emblem maybe?'

'Yeah – whatever. She was this huge ideer what sat over everybody's heads like a big flashin lectric sign, and not just Americans neither. Everybody. *Particularly* people who wanted to come here. She was this – emblem; that's it, Mac. Emblem of America. But that was before the movies, and if you stuck her in a picture now it would be lame.'

'So what are you thinking, you and Globe?'

'He don't think, at least in words, much. But his hands does plenty of gabbin. Enough for the both of us. He was thinkin if we could somehow capture a new image, some emblem for everythin, that would work on the silver screen, we could bust outta this small-time world an move on to better things. Get outta them bean counters' way. Bugge talks a good game about supportin his artists, but … well, that's what we want – doin it ourselves. An I think you might wanna help. You an that tasty lady of yours, wi these here articles in magazines.'

'Ok. I can see that. But the new thing, this bigger-than-Lady-Liberty draw that's going to knock my socks off, and my editor's too? What is it?'

'Take a look, boy, cause we're almost there. Right ahead, where the track drops down between them two escarpments, see?'

'Behind those trees, or bushes or whatever they are?'

'Yeah – right there. That's where we're headin. You'll see in a few minutes, then you'll understand.'

8

'Oh my God, Mr Globe,' said Stella, stepping out of McIntyre's car. They'd followed through the gap, parked alongside a ramshackle shed flanked by a stand of cactuses.

'Pete, please,' said Globe.

'Pete. My *God*.'

She gawked at the vast, sprawling sight, and he looked pleased, gestured towards her with one beefy hand.

'After you.'

9

McIntyre stood dumbfounded in front of the locomotive. In the middle of the desert, under a roasting sun, with nothing but weed and stumpy cactuses dotted here and there for fifty miles in any direction, it was so large he could stand in its cool and imposing shadow.

'The *new* New Colossus, right, Gene?' he said.

'Right.'

'So big it comes at you right out of the screen, striking out across the country into the endless west?'

'Right.'

'Like some sort of moving Lady Liberty, getting bigger every minute, impressing on the viewer the might and energy of America?'

'Right!'

Pratfall grabbed hold of a rail, grimaced for a moment at the heat sizzling his skin, then pulled himself up into the cab. 'All aboard!'

McIntyre wandered out of the shadow and back through blinding sun to where Globe and Stella leant against a stack of metal drums. Stella was working on a long cigarette, Globe fiddling with his sleeves, eyes downcast.

'Oh boy,' Mac said. 'Oh boy, oh boy.'

Stella laughed.

'Get your notebook out, feller. This here's a story heading your way.'

10

After a few hours the sun had declined, and they'd made a circuit of the entire camp. It was far longer and wider than the gash between the low rock humps suggested, and spread out like a dark pool across the floor of the desert. Someone – quite a few someones, by the look of it: Globe? Pratfall, their confederates? – had hacked apart loose earth across the whole of the space, stumping up cactuses and yanking the tangled roots of desert plants into piles around the borders. McIntyre could see, in the resulting wonky but hugely scaled-up baseball diamond, some purpose and element of design, but what sat atop the cleared ground made no sense to him at all.

In the immediate foreground, where Globe had hauled himself up and away – the giant locomotive chugging backwards along a pair of winking lines – was nothing but a buffer fashioned from several sawn-off sleepers, stacked side by side like pulled teeth, with dull grey mushrooms sprouting out of them like metal caps. That much figured; the thing had to stop somewhere, if nobody was to get hurt. But beyond the buffer lay a mass of intricate score marks – railway lines, he supposed – that branched and looped away in interlocking patterns as far as he could see. The metal, cold in the dim evening light, traced the sides of a wide circle around them, inside the diamond, radiating lines across its face like cuts in an orange, split exactly down the pith-lines.

Stella was sitting on an upturned crate by a pile of dry roots.

'Hey,' he said.

'Hey yourself.' She had a compact in one hand, a stick of kohl in the other. Her eyes appeared insufficiently racoony for the desert setting, and she reapplied deftly, asking the obvious questions without needing to look at him.

'So – what do you think?'

'I think the pair of them are crazy as loons. You?'

'Pretty much.'

He laughed and ran a finger around his damp collar. He wasn't sure he wanted to be here when the sun cranked up and that massive boiler started putting out steam.

'I do think it will be a great series, Mac. Don't you agree? I can imagine a dozen ways to spin it: little guys against the giants, artists getting out from under, curse of the money men, and so on. The pix will be marvellous. We'll need to get Davis out here right away.'

McIntyre paused. It certainly would be something, but he'd yet to free the notebook from his jacket pocket. His hands clenched and unclenched with uncertainty.

'Lemme ask you something,' he said. 'You seem to get along with old chunky, Globe, right?'

She nodded, snapping her compact and yawning.

'Well what's up with this thing? I got some of it out of Pratfall – a chance to pursue Globe's 'artistic vision' without having to bow to the whims of the studio, or something like that. I've no idea how they're going to make the money side work, and as far as I know, they're both under contract to Bugge, and he's no pushover. Did you see what he invested in that country-house short? They'd better get themselves a good lawyer. And what about the man himself? What did he say?'

'Oh, he's a sweet man, Mac. A lot sweeter than you. He doesn't say much, granted, but he talks a lot with his hands. A good listener can get to the heart of things.'

'A good listener?'

'Yes, Mac, a good listener. Did you know Mr Globe has been supporting his kids by helping other actors with the physical stuff, training and movement and whatnot, in his spare time?'

'His kids? Didn't know he was married.'

'See – that's what I mean. He's not, anymore. But still. Those hands convey a lot, if you know what I mean.'

McIntyre yawned himself, stood up.

'Alright, Stella – fascinating chat and all, but hadn't we better be getting back? It's a good couple of hours … '

'No, there's – ah, accommodation, for the crew tomorrow, a little kitchen and everything, on the other side. We're welcome to stay. In fact I think they *want* us to stay, and get a feel for what they're trying to do.'

McIntyre looked stunned. He had visions of an abandoned school bus jacked up on cinder-blocks, dirty cloth flapping in the wind and narrow stinking cots wedged in like sardines. But in the end it was okay. The duo seemed to have thought of everything: a small block of buildings, proper corrugated roofs, tables and beds you could sleep in. They looked as though they might have been here before, and put to new use. Some Army thing, maybe. For form's sake he grumbled about clothes and showers as Pratfall arrived in another car, one that presumably stayed on set, and ferried them about, but eventually he got used to the idea of a night in the desert, and took out his notebook over bourbon and cigars. It had a few leaves filled, but heaved with fat, virginal pages thirsty for ink. In wavering lantern-light he cornered the pair, questions at the ready.

'Mac, Mac – cool down, bub. We'll be ready in the morning, when the guys get here. You can ask us whatever you like.'

In the morning McIntyre woke alone. He had a throbbing head – boy, the novelty! – and an odd sense of fate, as though the day was poised on the edge of something momentous. He found a clay jar full of cold water in the kitchen, and the feeling soon departed.

Outside was a carnival. A dozen lean, wiry stagehands had materialised from nowhere, and were bustling around raising dust, hauling metal plates and beams on their shoulders, filling the trunk with cones and bolts of pale cloth, and talking non-stop while they moved. He shifted out of the way as a six-foot bruiser wobbled by bearing a girder-like strip of iron under both arms. He whistled sharply at the journalist, then disappeared round the corner. McIntyre shrugged and went back inside for the rest of his things.

On the wooden counter was a note: *Mac – whatcha doin still sleepin? Get yr ass over to the far side pronto! Straight out the door, right, little bit further on then right again and you're there. Can't miss – you'll know it when you get here.* It was signed Pratfall, though the letters had been scratched so hard into the back of a discarded garage bill, they'd dug into the paper, obscuring his signature.

McIntyre wondered if he needed a ride, but Gene seemed to think it was walkable, so he slipped the note into the back of his notebook and took another drink before he left.

It was cool in the shade of the walls, then the shadow of a long storage shed he hadn't noticed the night before, but when he stepped out into the sun it caught him like the back of a woman's hand. Sweat broke out on his forehead, stippled the back of his neck under the collar. He loosened his tie and followed a row of old sleepers laid out in fresh dirt. Outside, turn right; okay. Here he was. On a bit, right again – at this twisted tree stump, or whatever they called these damn things in the desert? The sleepers hooked right then dropped down a slight incline, and suddenly he knew he was in the right place.

It looked like a scene from some old-timey biblical epic – right down to the blasted desert and sky ranging on, mad and searing, for miles – but updated to the modern age, or at least the only modern age that counted: Pratfall's age of the train. In the centre of a great oval space lay a network of crazy, sprawling track – so massive it looked as though an engine could get up a head of steam then clatter round the circumference without needing to stop – with a bustling crowd of workers at its heart, manhandling equipment, raising plywood walls, sloshing paint about in great white buckets, everywhere laying down iron rails, tiny men in hand carts manipulating metal strips by means of mechanical arms hanging off the hand-trucks, the glinting strips dropping into place one after the other. New lines criss-crossed the space: lines, he assumed, that would let the great behemoth turn around and steam away into another shot, or back up out out of range for a suck at the overhanging rubber water-pipe that swayed in the distance.

Around the outside of the track were high walls, curving inwards and neatly placed within inches of each other. As he got nearer, he saw stage-hands tacking canvas sheets into place, pulling the white fabric till it stretched out taut and flat. He had no idea what they were for, but took a quick note in his book – *hoardings? screens, of some sort?* –

then picked up his pace. Beside the nearest sweep of rail was a crude tent pitched against the sun, and he could see workers passing in and out of its shadows, glasses winking in their hands. He beetled down the last of the rise and stuck his head inside.

'Hey, Mac! Glad you could join us.'

Pratfall reclined in a canvas chair, tall lemonade in hand.

'Yeah, yeah. Some operation you got here, Gene. Where's Globe, and Stella? Where did all these other guys come from?'

'Oh, we been recruiting them on the sly for months, gatherin all this junk together, too. Engine's not ours, but Globe's got a buddy knows some dude in the business, said we could borrow it for six months on a cost basis. Gotta pay the men, though, an that's addin up.'

'Are you serious? This is what, some sort of parallel company?'

'Naw, but don't tell Bugge anyway, Mac. It's strictly on the QT. What you might call an – ah, industry experiment.'

A quick wind got up and flapped the sides of the text. Pratfall gestured to a stand with a tin canister set up over a tap.

'Get yourself a drink; cool down. It's – well, you know. This thing's all Globe, at least the art, but I've bin sortin mosta the logistical stuff myself. Got the men on contingency, ya know. Not the busiest tima their year, an they was willin to take a little piece for their trouble. Me an Globe's on the best contingency of all. Nothin. If we get it out there when it's done that's us in the shit with every studio in America, so it'd better work, ya know?'

'And is it going to?'

'Course – acourse! Wouldn be here if it wasn't. Now, let's stop jawin and get out to the rails. Wanna show ya what I been talkin about the last few days. Wantcha ta see it in the flesh, so ta speak.'

McIntyre smiled, flipping open a page and brandishing his pen.

'Let's go.'

At the far curve of the oval, Pratfall pushed open two of the canvas-covered sidings and slipped in between. On the other side, McIntyre noticed they were mounted on small castors, and took note. Pratfall trundled them back together and the sudden shade was very welcome. Now they were inside the ring. Above them the sun burned on in a bright and uninterrupted wash of sky.

'Hot,' he said, dabbing his neck and brow with a damp handkerchief.

'Yep. Just the way Globe likes it.'

'Where is he, by the way? Supervising workers?'

'Naw – they don't need supervisin. They're mostly working with him for the sake of it, an a few greenbacks on the sly, like I said. He's up there yonder, with yer lady.'

McIntyre shielded his eyes and looked away to the cab of the mighty engine, stationed a few hundred yards away, facing the near side of the oval. Globe was indeed standing in the cab: a small, jerky version of his usual confident self, like the figures in those what-the-butler-saw machines his father told him about one drunken evening long ago – the figures' slightly shifty, fuzzy lines wavering back and forth in discernible action, despite their size. Stella's back was to the oval, Globe standing opposite and gesturing with his stick arms here and there. She reached out to touch his arm and Globe stopped dead, still as an automaton with its key wound down to nothing. She seemed to be wearing a pink blouse. How had she come by that?

'Hey Gene, we waiting for something here?'

'Yeah.'

Pratfall looked at his watch; it was just shy of ten o'clock, and he tapped the face with the end of one long finger to make sure it hadn't stopped. 'Ten on the nose, this baby's startin up and you're gonna see what we're made of.'

'What, with Globe and Stella up there, in the cab?'

'What, ya think that thing drives itself?'

'Well no, but I figured your train guy might have had – you know, an engineer to spare.'

'Naw. Globe's got it. He's had a few good practice runs while the boys was settin up, an I'm sure he has it down. Your gal wouldn't take no for an answer. Said she was fascinated, or some shit. Wanted to see him in action.'

'Him?'

'It, then – whatever. The beast. She's in for a ride, alright.'

McIntyre swallowed hard and raised an arm to wave in their general line of sight. Back and forth he waved, for half a minute, more, till his sleeve went limp, his muscles hot and hard. He thought his arm had disappeared in the mass of shimmer rising from the earth. But eventually Stella, small and bright as the bride on a cake, turned his way and waved back.

'*Alright*, then,' said Pratfall. He fished around in a battered leather bag and came out with a whistle. He gave three shrill blasts, and in the distance the tiny model Globe pulled on the engine's horn. Three great rumbling toots rolled across the intervening dirt.

'So now what?'

Pratfall pointed at the engine with a grin. Globe, who apparently had run through whatever preparatory stages were necessary to get the great iron monster rolling, now stood with his arm in the cab window – was it around Stella? – and their two small figures, pink and black, shifted slowly about as the engine started to move. McIntyre flinched, but knew a story when he saw one. He'd deal with the pair of them later. Pointing at the engine, the short run of track in front, the broad oval sweep of the stage dug round in the desert (for this was what it was, he realised; what it *must* be, the biggest, boldest stage for the world's biggest spectacle) he grabbed at Gene's sleeve.

'Do they come down front, then, and get on the circular track?'

'You bet.'

Gene didn't remove the journalist's arm, though even in the relative cool of the screen-walls his fingers seemed hotter than a brazier's breath. 'Done it a few times now. Globe works the thing till it gets up a head of steam, one of the fellers – there, look! standing by the switcher – slings him over to the big track, and then the thing belts round the oval like a dragon spittin fire.'

'Okay, but you know, so what? It's a big engine and all, but … '

'We run the films! Don't tell Bugge, but we lifted em from some piece-a-shit western for a coupla weeks. Hopin he won't miss em. They're views out the bumpy stagecoach window sorta things – on the screen it looks like yer pelting through the desert to hell knows where, San Fran or Seattle or someplace, who knows? But we loop it round and round till the audience's head pops right off, and they get their money's worth.'

McIntyre wanted to speak, but couldn't find the words; his fingers flew instead over the pages of the notebook, eyes moving up and down from page to engine, as it gained speed, then page once again. He watched his fingers blur, crudely capturing wheel and cab and cowcatcher as they started their lumbering journey round the far side of the oval. They hadn't reached a screen yet, though the figures in the cab were becoming a little clearer. Stella's pink blouse was bent at the waist, and if he could make out correctly, there was a black-clad arm moving underneath hers, the pair of them fiddling with something near the roof.

Suddenly the engine tooted, and his hand skidded through a half-assed diagram of the railway circuit. Pratfall laughed.

'Whoo, boy, you blow that thing!'

He took out his whistle and in response blew a high, sounding note over the roasting earth. Globe tooted again, and this time Mac saw – quite clearly – the soft pink slip of an arm drop over the black sleeve holding the string of the horn. They were perhaps three hundred yards off; no, not even that – the curve of the railway, the earth perhaps, must be distorting his vision. How could he see such detail at that distance? He jammed notepad and pen back in his pocket then grabbed again at Pratfall's sleeve.

'How long, Gene?'

'Don't worry – you'll get your spectacle, Mac! Keep on scribblin. Here they come!'

As the engine rounded the first corner of the loop, he saw a little man appear between the screens with a white flag fixed to the end of a pole; he dropped it, held still for second, then disappeared again behind a baffle-board. Pictures began to spring up along the curving walls (projected by another man, he assumed) but odd, huge and shaking in the unsettling silence, not smooth like on a theatre screen, as though they formed some rough organic segment of the landscape, rather than an illusion: hot morning suns, little different from the day (save for that wobble); long shots of a fixed horizon passing a window, the occasional bobble of a cactus-top or scrub bush puncturing the monotony; here and there a water tank – he recognised that ridged grey elephant's trunk of the feeder hose – and a motley collection of weathered buildings, bumping quickly through, passing out of shot.

'Hah!'

He squinted slightly and things resolved themselves to a settled picture, the true vibration of the pounding desert. Suddenly he wished he was up there, in the cab, pink blouse be damned. The engine was rounding the second corner, now, passing the curved screens and joggling pictures. The drivers tooted the horn in a long blast of joy. Pratfall slapped the journalist on the back.

'Here it comes, boy – heading our way. Getcha peepers on. It's the past, but it's the future, too!'

As the engine turned into the straight, Mac realised this was the home stretch, and smiled. The notebook slipped back effortlessly into his hands, and he took up the scene without missing a stroke.

The engine loomed, high and grey and imposing. Behind Pratfall, who had stood to his full height in the slim shade of the screens, eyes wide as though this was all new, the full spectacle unbeheld till this very hour – McIntyre knew he was a showman, and full of shit, but nonetheless the excitement seemed genuine – Mac had to step aside and around the taller man to get a proper look. Here it came, then! A few years back, before the advent of sound, there would have been some crazed saloon-bar tickler hammering out a rhythm to accompany the increasing presence of the train, but here, over the hot endless space of the desert, its rhythms grew unassisted, multiplying crazily over and over in the dead air, until his mind was filled with the kick and rattle of thumping metal, the whoosh of steam. In the cab, the drivers, arms mingled in who knew what seedy combination, pulled the cord again and didn't let go.

Here it came – Gene's great, mobile show, the greatest thing since Lady Liberty; better, even! Those poor, benighted peasants, sailing half-starved into New York harbour, limp after months below decks, crawled in slow motion past the grand dame of welcome; here the continent itself thundered past, smashing into their eyes and reverberating through the fragile bones of their ears with all the unstoppable glory of America.

Globe and Pratfall were right. The screens behind the hammering engine spiralled up, round and away, their juddering images blending like scenes glimpsed from a great gay carousel, calliope tootling mellifluously overhead, candied delights of light and space bobbing up around them in a throng. He threw down his notebook and raised his hands, clasping Gene's in congratulation, waving at the cab as it hurtled by huge and bellow-loud, tremendous, the stink of hot coal fizzing like champagne in his nostrils.

But here – what was this? Beyond their two pairs of hungry eyes, all teary with joy, the wheels began to clash and squeal as the engine turned into the final loop, gearing up for home and a thunderous run to victory. Through the cab windows, for half a second, building-tops flashed by then were gone, replaced by unending blue. Pink and black were a blur, now, as a harsher note crept in – McIntyre registered sudden sparks, hot and not unexpected, but surely a few moments early for their final, cresting run?

Gene jumped out of the screen's shadow. He grabbed backwards for McIntyre, and his hand found the notebook, seized it in a sweaty grasp.

'No, Mac – no!'

But it was apparent, before he could respond, that the world was serving up a huge and sonorous yes. The notebook squeaked between clutching nails and dropped to the dirt. McIntyre jumped forward, batting away Pratfall's hands, as they flailed uselessly after the cab. Now sparks had bloomed into clouds of fire, misty and violent as the early stars, and were engulfing the cab; pink-and-black was nowhere to be seen. Instead, the vast grey side of the engine began to fold up like a squeezebox as the train hurtled too quickly into the turn, and its wheels left the rails.

McIntyre and Gene stood together, hands limp, jaws agape, as the spectacle of the century rammed itself down the line, turning, flipping up like a snake bursting from a funny kid's can of nuts, and ramming through the curved screens in a spiral of flame. As he watched an errant wheel take off a workman's head, McIntyre turned to his companion, but the tall man lay flat on the ground, eyes twitching white.

'I, I – ' he said. 'I – '

A breeze lifted a handful of sparks in his direction. One caught on the notebook's cover, puffing it up with fire. He reached out, across a space as cold as the universe, before the flames could touch the tips of Pratfall's senseless fingers.

On Sugarloaf Hill

1

IT ALWAYS SEEMED to me that he had lived in Ainthorpe forever. Edward's little house, wedged between one end of a terrace and the large house on the corner, was narrow and not particularly long; at the back it ended in a tumbledown garden, which followed the back hill to a small beck choked with weeds, and at the front squeezed itself down to a tiny front yard giving on the main road. His front window looked out at the farm buildings opposite. The side window was so grimed with soot, you could barely make out the alley running the length of the house, where he had been rumbling his rubbish-and-cinder bins for more than forty years. The place felt as though it had grown up around him, that he nestled – perfect as a conker in its half-cracked shell – opposite a constantly burning fire.

'Oh, no, Abigail,' Aunty Jean said. 'He lived for more years in Westerdale than he did here, and in a lot posher house, too.'

I was back from the first term of my middle year at university. She and my mother were fussing round, making Edward comfortable, arranging things just so, but though he didn't say much, I suspected he'd rather no one noticed him turning ninety.

When I arrived, he looked up from his lap and smiled, putting down a letter on his side-table and starting to rise.

'No, Edward! No you don't.'

I gave him a big hug right in his chair. He'd never stood on ceremony, insisting everyone call him by his given name, but at his age it was probably a relief for the world to come to you – if you still had much interest in it – rather than scurrying around the place in a constant flap.

‘Hello, love,’ he said.

‘Hi. You’re looking well. Aunty Jean looking after you?’

He looked around a bit conspiratorially, then smiled again.

‘Course. Wish she’d give up this birthday malarkey, mind. Your mother too.’

‘I know. Still, nice to see everyone, don’t you think?’

‘Happen it is.’

The room was warm, with a slight smoky smell; sounds of women moving around the kitchen came through the hatch now and then, one knock and pot-clink at a time, and mingled with the muffle of voices. He looked sleepy. By the time I’d got my coat off and was properly settled, I didn’t get chance to ask who his letter was from.

He lay his head on the high chair-back, two gingery-white sprigs of his remaining hair folded down like fox’s ears, and off he went.

2

They held the party in the early afternoon in deference to Edward’s age – and the likelihood he might be asleep before evening – so by teatime the house was quiet. Aunty Jean and my mother popped up to the Fox & Hounds for a drink. I finished washing the last of the pots, dried the pans and hung them on their hooks, then took off Edward’s tiny striped pinny (which barely reached to my waist) and sat down in the armchair opposite. Edward nodded.

Since I went to university, I’ve tried to write to him once a week. He has a phone, but doesn’t like to use it. Last time I was here I brought my laptop to finish some notes for an essay. He leant over and poked at the back of the cover. It creaked, folded a bit.

‘Computer, is it?’

'That's it. I charge it up by plugging it in the wall, then I can carry it round and work anywhere I want. I write my essays in the park, sometimes!'

He shook his head, but made no comment.

'I could write my letters on this, if you like, then print them out and send them?'

'Nay, lass. I like your handwriting. Reminds me of when I was young. I never used to like making entries in ledgers, but I always enjoyed writing letters.'

He pointed at a stack of correspondence on the side-table, beside a coaster with its tall, skinny coffee cup and a bottle of whisky, its level mysteriously similar to my last visit. The letter he was reading yesterday was folded on top. It looked to be written on expensive paper, and the fold was sharp as a knife blade.

For a few minutes, neither of us spoke. The low crackle of a log comfortably filled the silence.

'What's your essay about, then?'

'Eh? Oh, the Victorians, you know.'

'Brontës, *Dracula*, all that?'

'Well, not just them, but yes. That period.'

'Came out three years before I were born, you know – *Dracula*. Bits of it set in Whitby, too, if I remember – up on the East Cliff, round the Abbey.'

'Really?'

'Oh, yes. Quite the heritage we've got round here.'

He laughed and ran a hand across his bald head, then through the rough crinkles behind his ears. 'Bet your lecturers told you nowt about that, did they?'

As a matter of fact, they hadn't. One listened to my essays in respectful silence – I knew I was doing well when the ash on his forgotten Rothman's fattened beyond the point of gravity – and the other cited his own work seventeen times in one edited volume. So much for him. I'd never thought much about how North Yorkshire appeared to the world, but then I was only nineteen. There was time enough for everything.

'Sat up on the shelf, it did, where I couldn't reach. Fat looking yellow thing. I think my parents were scared I might read a bit.'

'Were they?'

'Oh, aye. They were quite protective in them days. I was only one of two boys, and my elder brother got killed in the war. That made em worse.' He smiled, and the net of wrinkles around his eyes moved like twigs nudging round a slow-moving stream. 'Expect your mam's a bit that way, isn't she?'

'Well, she was. Trusts me more these days, what with my being out on my own – most of the time, anyway. She's letting me have her old car, the Micra. I'm taking it back down with me.'

He smiled again, patted my hand. His palm had a dry, slightly raspy quality.

'Reckon you'd like to give me a ride, then, on your maiden voyage?'

'Absolutely! Where do you want to go?'

'Well I don't get out much these days. How about everywhere?'

'Everywhere it is.'

3

We started early, toting a flask of milky coffee Aunty Jean insisted we take, together with a few ham and pease-pudding sandwiches.

'Make sure you keep him fed and watered,' she said.

'He's not a pony!'

'Never you mind. Just do as I say.'

I saluted, accepting the canvas bag and taking Edward's arm. It was a crisp, sunny winter's day, and he was dressed as usual in a three-piece suit, a new-looking hat held under his arm, his watch on its chain and nestled in his pocket.

'Bit late, aren't yer?' he said.

'Alright – let's get going.'

In the passenger seat he got settled, the hat – briefly in its rightful place – now parked on one knee. I jostled the bag around till it sat, within easy reach, between his feet.

'Now, where do you really want to go?'

He thought for a minute, scratching his ear.

'Let's start with Westerdale.'

'Westerdale it is.'

I carefully backed the car – *my* car! – out of the spot between Jean's Subaru and the dry stone wall, checked both ways, then did a three-point turn till we were facing the right way and set off. As the Nissan climbed out of Ainthorpe, passing Danby School (which seemed to have been spruced up since I was there, the perimeter wall newly-pointed, roof slates sparkling) I took the bend that passed the monumental stonemason's. Edward nodded in that direction and lifted his hand slightly from his lap.

'Few tales there, in my day,' he said.

'Oh, yeah?'

But he just nodded and smiled. We slowed for the steep bank past the war memorial, waiting at the bottom for a lumbering green bin-lorry to pass, then took a left for Castleton, and he did it again.

'Ellerstang. The stories we used to hear.'

I'd been intrigued by the big house myself – the way it seemed to loom out, all front, then shrink back into its diamond windows when you passed, like a spectre in one of those Edwardian tales they told round the fireside at Christmas. I waited, changing down a gear, but he seemed to have nothing more to offer.

We hit Castleton high street and kept going, past the village shop, the blocky fortress of the police house, to where the top road forked and we had a choice of paths to Westerdale. The sun was poking through, so I went right, past the gravel pits and the rugged drop to the far side of the valley. The road wound down in a series of sharp knots, with sheep rambling right up to the window and wonky fence posts leaning over the road. I thought it might spark a memory of two. I imagined him reaching out to boop a sheep's nose, the waft of grassy tod-piles, or the rustling of bushes up close.

On the far side, the valley dropped away in a series of looping curves. I pulled my visor down against the sun, leaned over to get Edward's, but he was already popping out the little rounded bracket from its housing. Soon the road narrowed to a track and we slowly nosed down the hill. There were sheep alongside, but seemingly too busy cropping grass to pay any attention to a small passing car. Edward wound down his window and looked out, but didn't say anything. At the final turn before we hit the valley floor, began the shallow couple-of-mile climb into Westerdale, he started to point things out.

'Used to buy from that farm,' he said.

'Which one?'

The indicator was tick-tocking madly as I joined the road.

'There, on the rise' he said, between tickings.

'You'll see – oh, here we are, bit further on. The one down the lane, too.'

'What were you doing, Edward?'

'I was an agricultural agent for the squire. He had all this land – great-grandson still does, I'd imagine – but it was too much to manage, to keep on top of, you know, so he employed a manager, and the manager employed me.'

'Did you have to go to university for that?'

He laughed. A crow hopped out of the way as we entered a dip, and the car laboured up the other side.

'I was out of school at fourteen, lass, and earning me keep right away. University!'

He kept up a stream of chortles till we entered Westerdale, taking a left and meandering through the village and out of the top, where I pulled over into a rough layby in the shadow of Sugarloaf Hill. I thought we could take in the view, maybe, then have a sandwich or two.

'If I'd lived in town, I would have been a gas-fitter or summat. But we lived out here. I washed pots for a while at the Downe Arms, laboured on one of the farms, did stock work for the Co-op an all. I didn't start on the agenting stuff till I was almost twenty.'

'When was that, Edward?'

He didn't scratch his head or count on his fingers. With the hill brooding above us, a great slab of moorland – just the blunt end of the moor, really, not a hill proper – jutting out over the village like an angry brow, sun spilling here and there over the bracken, he seemed to know right away.

'1920, lass. Queer old time it was, too.'

4

Perkins, the squire's factor, called us in one by one, I remember.

No ceremony; nowt like that. He'd put out the word around the villages – never mind who he worked for, he had work in 'the agricultural trade' for an enterprising young lad. Turn up at such-and-such a time in the back parlour of the Arms if you were interested.

Well, it being only a couple of years after the war, there weren't that many young lads fit enough, or well enough in the head, to take on those sort of duties, and for such a – well, Abigail, you'll ave to forgive me French, but for such a colossal prick as Perkins. Even the hosses hated him, high-stepping lordly bastard that he was.

I'd had friends, only a couple of years older than me, who got dragged off to the trenches and came back missing bits of themselves. Legs, arms. One lad had an eye blown out by shrapnel. Another screamed his head off every time he saw a curtain twitching in a breeze, or something scratching at a door. Rats and shadows, he said.

Anyway, turns out all the villages round could muster only five or six lads worth having: all my age, too young to have been yanked over to France, too stupid to avoid getting into Perkins' clutches.

He had us on the sinner's bench – you know, that one people leave their umbrellas on now, but in my day it was where the drunks used to try and hold on to the floor before they staggered off into the night. One by one we went in, there was a few minutes of mumbling, then we came out again. My turn arrived and my heart was up thick as a rabbit's in my throat. I pushed open the half-door and went over to him, cap-in-hand, bowed my head.

'I'm interested in the position, sir,' I said. I tried to sound humble but energetic; like somebody who'd work and not give his lord-and-master any trouble, you know.

He looked me up and down, eyes raking over me like tank-tracks, then waved me out again without saying owt. A few minutes later he came to the sinner's bench and pointed at me, then waved off the other lads and disappeared back inside. I looked around, followed him through.

'D'you know why I chose you – ah, Braithwaite?'

'No, sir?'

'You were the only one who bothered to shine his shoes. Not that it matters – you'll be knee-deep in cow-shit, in no time at all. Come on.'

And away I went, meek as a lamb, to my first day's work. These are the things life turns on, lass!

5

The first few months were hard; I'm not going to tell you any different. Perkins was everything everybody'd said he was, and then some. I enjoyed my pay-packet, but that was about it. (Even then, I had to hand it over to me mother lock-stock-and-barrel, just like me dad, and we both got our pocket money back for the week.) I spent more time with my pals in the snug, mithering about Perkins, than I ever did enjoying meself. What a waste of time! I'm amazed they stuck with me, those lads, but they did. Both dead now, of course, the rest taken by the next war.

Where was I?

Oh, right you are – those first few months. I soon got the idea that when the man said training, learning the role, all that, what he meant was taking the bits of his job what he hated, or thought beneath him, and passing them on – like a conveyor belt, you know, only the stuff rumbling my way had been bashed into the worst possible shape. I just had to lump it and get on with things.

When he said cow-shit, mind, he was nothing less than completely truthful. I used to get home from a day touring the barns and my mother would wrinkle her nose, waft her fingers in front of her face.

'I can't help it, mam – it's cows, and cows has to live somewhere, like everyone else!'

'*Why*, Edward – surely there's more to it than shovelling that – well, *that*, around here and there, to get a better look at what's underneath. Can't those farmers help you understand? Do they not have buckets?'

I laughed, she looked pained, and then I laughed again, feeling not one single shred of guilt. She kept a nice house, but also took most of my pay to do it. I didn't come home and torture her; don't get that idea. But I must say, the look on her face kept a little bit of fun alive in me for those first few months of torture.

I thought it would never end, that I'd be stuck in this smelly hell for ever, learning nothing, when there came a message of sorts, from above. He was out one day, in the trap – Perkins – and he grabbed the whip from the driver (Calum told me later – he was a Scotch lad, passing through, really, but a miracle with horses) as if they needed driving hard round a corner.

Well he drove em hard, that's for sure, and they panicked and skipped the traces as they came out of the bend. It's just where we stopped, you know, by the big house on the corner. Wasn't much more than a crossing-place in the dirt back then. But he *knew best*, you see, so he careered em on at speed all the way round and they broke out and tipped the pair of them into the fence. Callum landed on all fours – like a cat, he said – in the turf. But Perkins, he was older, heavier, and he sort of flew like a fat arrow into the gate post, head-on. Split his skull from top to bottom.

It was a nine-days' wonder, then life got back to normal, the way things always did. The squire acquired himself a new factor, and I got a new boss. A good one, this time. Things changed again.

'Heard what happened to Perkins,' the new feller said the first morning.

I mumbled something deferential, but he wasn't having it. Mr Smith – plain, sturdy and reliable, like a good hammer; that was him. Nonsense and Smith didn't mix.

'Speak up, lad, if you want to work with me. I heard about it, but there's nothing can be done. Knew him a bit, too, and I don't suppose you'll be too deep in mourning, now will you?'

'Can't say that I will, sir, no.'

'Good. Well, that's that out of the way. What's he been having you do?'

So I told him.

He turned away, muttering. I couldn't lay my hand on the Bible and give my testament in court, but there was some swearing going on there, I'm sure.

'Alright, then – alright,' Smith said after a minute. 'As I said, the past's the past. There's no fixing it, and no point trying. We'll go on from today like I'd interviewed you yesterday, and tomorrow was your first day. You understand me?'

I did, and I followed him for nigh on thirty years, in the end.

That day we simply toured. It was refreshing, accompanying a neat man in straightforward tweeds and cap – brogues on his feet! – to be reintroduced to the many farmers, auctioneers, hauliers and storagemen I'd previously met, only not in the guise of dogsbody and muck-raker. There were a few muddy episodes, I'll grant you, but by the end of the day I felt as though I had gained three feet, and my shoes were still clean – or if not clean, at least not plastered with cow-muck and all the worst scrag-ends of the farmyard.

‘I think I can see a future in this, mam,’ I said when I got home. She peered over her reading glasses at my suit (still presentable), my cap – a bit windswept, she noted – and at last, the blessed shoes.

‘They won’t take more than a minute to buff clean in the morning, Arnold,’ Mam said. My father just grunted from his chair beside the fire. For some reason peculiar to my mother’s upbringing, shoes and all activity associated with them were a father’s domain, alone; I’ve no idea why.

She smiled, took out her purse.

‘Here.’

I smiled back, and in a rush of delight, treated myself to an extra jar that evening. I’d a lot to learn, but one thing was for certain – don’t ever look a gift horse in the mouth!

6

A few weeks later, Smith had introduced me to most of the principal folk in the job; I’d got used to a higher level of work, using my mind and nous, really, rather than just my back; and my mother was loving the cleanliness of my shoes, as well as a bit of a rise in pay. I felt bright and energetic, when I rose in the cold house and got the fire going before the rest of them. Keen, as I pulled the door closed on a single lamp, sniffing the air for some sense of the weather, then trekked down the lane and through the silent village to the cross-roads in the dip. For some reason, Smith liked to wait in his trap at the point Perkins went to his doom, and who was I to argue?

One morning in October, he was waiting with the reins loose, as usual, but instead of my stepping up, he stepped down and stood with one hand on the horse’s flank.

‘Braithwaite,’ he said.

'Sir.'

'How many times, lad – just Smith.'

'Yes, sir.'

He sighed, but smiled, too. His beard was growing out for the winter, and I noticed a few threads of silver amongst the curly russet-browns. He rubbed his cheeks and stamped a bit in the chill. The sun was up, somewhere, but hadn't yet reached the cross-roads. Smith pointed back in the direction of Castleton high street, then twirled his hand in the direction beyond.

'Change of plan today, lad. We were going to go into Whitby, meet Snaithe, like I told you Saturday, but summat's come up. Master's had an – well, enquiry, I suppose, of sorts. Don't know much, but we've to spend the day in Westerdale searching out something for a gentleman returning to these parts. Needs something small, but nice, and we'll certainly be able to accommodate him, the master says. Well I don't know about that, but we will do our level best. Hop in, then, lad. You can drive.'

This was new!

I took the reigns, flicked the pony briskly up the hill and over the cobbled high street; around the top-bend; onto the rutted track that dropped down the far side of the hill, then wound its way for a few miles along the bottom and climbed up gradually into Westerdale. The light increased as we made our way, and by the time we took the last turn into the village, it was standing bright as an apple skin against the blank grey sky. We slowed gradually, till we crunched over the inn's forecourt and handed off the horse, then set out on foot.

'What exactly are we looking for?'

'Well, the gentlemen wasn't overly specific.'

He rummaged in his breast pocket for a moment, coming out with a small notebook and a pair of spectacles. I smiled as he hooked them over his ears and peered at the notebook, riffled through its pages.

'Well – here, look. Accommodation, the squire says. Commodious but not luxurious; need not be centrally-located; must be adjacent to running water; need not have its own track; privacy – indeed isolation – a must. Does that description spark anything in you, Braithwaite, with your knowledge of the dale?'

Oddly enough, it did.

When I was a child, I'd spent some time in Westerdale. My aunt and uncle had a farm at the far end of the dale, and my brothers and I were left with them when my parents had to go into Whitby for some occasion or other. Once we built a kite from split-sticks, string and waxed paper filched from the farmhouse kitchen. I held the braces down while Tom splinted the spine, pulled the cord tight and checked its tension. Davey ran out the spool of line, after tying it off on the rag-tail, till it was fifty yards long, and we ran with it up the side of the moor towards Sugarloaf Hill.

'It's not really a hill, you know – not as such. More the end of something – a big wedge where the moor up top rises into a prominence, then falls away. From down here it looks like the side of a sugarloaf, like at the co-op.'

He nodded.

'And this kite of yours?'

'Oh – yes, sir. Mr Smith, I mean. Well we ran it as fast and as far as we could up the dale side, past the big oak then alongside the dry stone wall, over the track there, till we were in the shadow of the hill. The wind kept puffing and spurting, and we were hopeful of getting a lift, but when we ran it out to the full length of the string, it would die down again. We were disappointed – angry, almost. All that work!

Eventually Tom hit on the idea of running it along the spine of the Hill, letting what wind there was pick it up as it whooshed up and over. It worked, too – for a while.'

Mr Smith refolded his spectacles, returned the notebook to his pocket.

'Delightful as your childhood tale is, lad, what bearing has it on our present business?'

'Oh, well. On our way up we cut across a rough track, you see, out this way – over yonder, actually. You'll see it in a minute. There's a small cottage by a stand of trees, and somebody piped the spring down to it from the moor. If it's still there, I thought it might do the gentleman nicely.'

He patted his pockets as though he'd lost something of importance, but whatever it was, he soon forgot it when we passed through the last of the bends out of the village, trees hanging hard and brittle on each side, and the cottage came into view.

The track had clearly not been used for some time. Its mouth lay off the main road over the moor. At some period, long past, it had been worn down to flat earthen ruts by cartwheels trundling back and forth, but as we took it, the dirt was thick and crusted with moorland debris. Even the crude turning circle in front of the cottage was almost gone, drifted under a score of dusty summers, clabbered up, rutted and frozen till it cracked apart in spring. It did not look promising, and I kept my eyes down, away from my boss. He was springing ahead, though – looking at the curve of imposing moor that jutted above, walking up to the cottage door and striking it with the butt of his stick, joggling the window frames; in short, subjecting this small and forgotten dwelling to inspection with an expert eye.

After a few moments he set off at a brisk trot around the building. The trees alongside – these looked healthy, at least – rustled pleasantly in the breeze, and when the branches were at rest, I could hear the trickle of water, directed down the moor from somewhere above. I walked up the hill a short way and found a black metal tank embedded in the soil. I lifted out a number of branches, some dry bracken, then kicked at piles of scrub that lay over the pipe, giving it a tap. It seemed solid, and was cool to the touch. The moving tickle of water sounded from within.

'Braithwaite!'

Smith had reappeared, and was beckoning me to the front door of the cottage.

'To whom does this belong?'

'No idea, sir – though I suspect Crane at the inn will know.'

'I think with some work it may suit the squire's purposes. Get away to the inn, then lad, and ascertain to whom we should apply.'

I nodded and set off back to the village at a lick. I left Smith outlined against the moorland and the white sky, hand on hip, one hand pushing the brim of his hat over a damp forehead. A small fire lit in my belly as I reached the inn. If this opportunity proved out, it would certainly be to my credit, and to my boss's, too – surely something would come of it.

I straightened my tie as I walked (actually, scuttled would be a better way to put it) snapped my waistcoat tight and knocking the mud from my boots, went into The Marker to find out what we needed to know.

7

I've maybe made things sound easy, but only in an effort to keep it moving along. A lot of my job, it turned out, was what you young ones call research – unearthing facts and bits of knowledge, some written down nice and neat, some lodged in a particular person's head like a burr stuck on the back of your calf, where you can't see the damn thing. I found out who owned the cottage, all right – told Smith right quick, too – but seeing as I was on a learning track, he said, the job of chasing the name down to anything useful as a proposal, offered and accepted, was mine alone, and the devil's own job, it turned out to be.

It had once belonged to a farmer, like most things. But he'd died, sometime back in the 1880s, and had a son, who inherited, but who was away at sea. *He'd* died in his turn years back, only no one knew exactly where or when, and after I got the name from Crane the barman – quite free with it, he was, though his lip curled a bit at the end of his dispensing this knowledge – everything seemed rosy. Not so. He'd had a wife, somewhere down south in a port town, and she'd left things in the hands of a firm of solicitors. *They'd* kept everything to themselves, perhaps hoping for some future bounty when land went up, or something like that, but when I used the squire's name in my letter and pried her name out of them – like a bag of clams, they were, the awkward buggers – she shook out the secret pretty quick, said she'd had nothing from the old sod worth having, and she'd be delighted to let the squire have it on a long lease for a very reasonable sum.

Well, that was fine, then – only it took nigh on two months of back and forth to winkle this out of the various parties, and Smith was on me every week for news of progress. It was a blessing to be able to let him know we could proceed, now the snow was here and the dale thickly coated with it, like a beautiful heavy blanket. Marvellous! Life sometimes gangs up on you, love; remember that.

Smith left it to me to arrange the work, with local lads, mostly – checking the roof, windows and floorboards (some needed taking up and replacing, and they found a rat's nest in one corner – I'll spare you the details); making sure the water ran, and had nowt but a bit of rust in it; hacking away the scrub and freeing the turning circle for the gentleman's trap. We were done by spring, and Mr Smith gave the squire a glowing report. He seemed pleased. The gentleman wished to take occupancy in early summer, he said, when the light cast its favour upon the long dale, almost as though it could never die (I do remember these phrases; quite peculiar, they were, but they linger).

After a ploughman's and a pint of ale one Friday in May, my boss leant back in his chair and put his arms behind his head.

'So, Braithwaite. All done, if not quite dusted, eh?'

'How do you mean, Fred?'

After six months' decent, unstinting work, he had allowed me to use his Christian name, when it was just the two of us. I ran the list of tasks through my brain faster than a book-keeper totting up his numbers, and couldn't think of a single blessed thing I'd left undone. I took a final swallow, shook my head.

'How do you mean?'

He pointed back over my shoulder, through the leaded window and across the gravel to the wedge of Sugarloaf Hill.

'You did the work – you'll want to welcome the gentleman, see his needs are met, won't you?'

8

It took a few weeks, but in a number of letters back and forth – forwarded through a firm of Whitby solicitors, this time, and delivered rather splendidly in their own cart – we established that the gentleman in question would arrive to take up residence in the cottage on the twenty sixth of June.

I didn't have a name for the cottage (perhaps he'd give it one), nor the gentleman himself, come to that; peculiar, I admit, but not something at the age of almost twenty-one that bothered me over much. The night before, I laid my suit on the clothes-horse to air.

'You look happy,' my mother said. 'This new feller seems to be doing you good.'

She came up behind me, ruffled my hair.

'Don't wear the grey tie with that.'

Then she went to bed. I sat by the range a few minutes longer. She'd just blacked it that morning, and the metal had a depth I enjoyed for its strange disappearing act. Sit for a moment, and stray thoughts were drunk down into the leading like some refreshing draft, and any worries right after them. I watched as one lone coal broke open, dropped end over end towards the grate. I shifted my boots, placing the top one bottom-most, but still didn't move. I don't know if I had any sense of moment; that might be a bit much. I preferred getting out, and on, to mithering over anything inside me. I like people who are the same. But now I smiled, and closed my eyes, and let the warm black hearth absorb everything.

Next morning I was out before the rest of the household stirred.

The sun was up, burning off dew on the roof-slates and garden blooms, sparkling in the rain-butts, and steaming away the damp from the night before. I tightened my laces on the stair, then stepped away, bread-and-dripping in hand, for the walk to Westerdale. Two miles, three at most – nothing, really, and a bright sky to cheer me on my way.

I whistled as I walked through the village and over the top, following the twisting track down to the bottom of the valley. The sheep were up – though they looked a bit creaky, and the lambs weren't much better, breath pushing out in the keen air – and as the sun warmed everything up, I saw a few other animals out. A late fox, surprised beside the stile, dived for cover under a thicket; a pair of crows bickered on a five-bar gate, and as I approached the village marker, a huddle of beasts lowed at me when I passed. Their breakfast was still a ways off, I thought.

There were a few people around as I passed. Each gave me the usual morning nod, then went about their business. I topped out of the village and took the side track leading to the cottage where the road bent away across the moor, underneath Sugarloaf Hill.

I had asked – in vain, in turned out – for a pocket-watch at Christmas, so had no way to tell what time I arrived, but placed my backside on the outdoor bench (Fred and I had pulled it from a stand of weeds, over by the tank) and made ready to wait. Another crow cawed, then flapped off as he seemingly took offence to me. In a while the low, plinking runnel of the water trickling down the moor became all I could hear. It was soothing, as I sat; lulling, even. The morning passed, and I dabbed my brow now and again as the sun crested. I took off my jacket, then my waistcoat, and finally my tie. What would my mother think of my sitting here practically naked, waiting on a gentleman!

Mother be blowed. It was positively warm, now, and the notion crept up on me that he might not come till the sun had dropped back down the sky – or come at all.

It was late when it happened, and the sun *had* gone, indeed – or perhaps just edged below the horizon. I could still make out little more than shadows. First a distant crunching, like the grinding of bones in an old fairy tale, then more distinct: pops and rolls, as of new wheels down a gravelled track. Then the crack of a whip, and here he came – a figure fit for the waiting.

I stood and quickly pulled on waistcoat and jacket, ran my tie back up my throat, slicked back my hair over a damp brow.

The cart came down the track, swung wide in the turning circle, and stopped, horse panting, driver standing tall on the footplate with an audible creak. He rose to his full height and surveyed everything about him, then stepped down. His foot touched the gravel in silence. I whipped off my cap and bowed.

'Mr Braithwaite, I presume?' the man said.

'Yes, sir. Edward Braithwaite, on behalf of the squire, and factor Smith, to welcome you to – well, to your cottage, sir.'

There was a short pause, as he slipped off first one glove then the other, revealing long, slim brownish fingers.

'I thank both you and the squire most effusively. Your Mr Smith, also. Will you lead the way?'

Well, I bowed again, lass, and did as he bade me.

We started for the door.

9

The maid we'd hired to clean the cottage, give it a decent airing – and the painter who touched things up here and there – had both done a spiffy job. Inside, it was small but homely. She'd left a few sprays of flowers around, magicked a tablecloth and some other bits and pieces for furniture so it felt lived in. (The squire himself had interested himself in the project sufficiently to empty a labourer's cottage elsewhere on the estate, and send over what might be needed.)

'Here we are, then, sir,' I said. 'Your place. I hope it's to your liking.'

He laid his hat and gloves on the table, took a look around. I noticed his height against the long white square of the window – well over six feet, I thought; much bigger than me, anyway! – and the limber, almost sinuous way he moved. His limbs seemed supple, his movements always in harmony with themselves and their surroundings. It's funny, but after a minute I could hardly imagine him anywhere else.

'Yes indeed, Mr Braithwaite. It certainly is. You have done a sterling job of preparation.'

'Please, call me Edward, sir.'

'Very well – I shall call you Edward. I understand that the 'you' undertaking these preparations has been almost entirely *you*, singular, as in you, yourself – has it not?'

'Well sir, Mr Smith – he's my boss, for the squire, you know – and Alice the maid helped, too. Oh, and Reggie, the bodger for the estate. He trimmed, painted and whatnot. But I did do a lot myself, yes, sir.'

He smiled.

'I believe I owe you a debt of gratitude. However, I am somewhat tired from my journey, and wish to rest. Would you do me the honour of uncoupling my horse, parking the trap to one side of the turning circle you have provided, and taking the animal for its sustenance and shelter at the inn?'

'Of course, sir. It will be my pleasure.'

'And I wish you to return tomorrow – in the afternoon, at around this same time, when the sun has set, if you will.'

'Yes sir? How else can I be of service?'

'Oh, there are a number of things. But I wish simply to tell you of my gratitude more fully, in coming here, and finding a – home, so well-equipped. I wish merely to thank you properly, Mr Braithwaite.'

'Edward, sir.'

'Yes indeed. Edward. I wish to thank you in my own way, but for the moment – '

I knew he wanted to be alone, and bowed out of the little room, slipped on my cap and unharnessed the horse. I heard the door close gently behind me, the bolt sliding into place. As I set off down the hill with the horse, I began to whistle.

10

People like to talk, lass. You'll find that. Gab and natter and prattle on something fierce, especially in the country; you're probably that way when you're around other young uns. But back then there was no television, no radio or computers like you have now, nor anything much beyond the paper and a book or two.

What they did was talk.

I was besieged by my mother as soon as I got in the door.

'Alright – alright! Lemme get me boots off, will you?'

But I was laughing as I said it. She sat, as she usually did, with knitting in her lap, a cup of weak tea at her elbow, and the dog curled up somewhere under her skirts. Either there or on the hearth. I never knew such a lazy hound. My mother leant forward gently, so as not to disturb him, but quite intently all the same.

'Well?'

'Well what?'

'What's this high and mighty fellow like, then? You've been skivvying for him for months – was it worth the candle?'

I could have reminded her that the work had been far more interesting – stimulating, really – than anything Perkins ever had me do, and also involved considerably less cow-muck, a subject on which she was hardly ever silent, but it didn't really seem worth it. I was happy, and intrigued, so I just told her what I thought.

Mother sat for a minute after I was done, musing. She took a small sip of tea (it had to be cold; she hadn't refreshed it in quarter of an hour) and setting down her needles, put both hands on her knees.

'Now, Edward,' she said. 'Are you sure you've told me everything?'

'Yes, Mam – why wouldn't I?'

'Well, I don't rightly know. Only you young ones never do.'

She'd pinned me like a corkboard moth with her steely eye.

'Mind you do, when there's owt worth knowing.' I just nodded.

She had no idea, nor I, how much more there would be to tell.

11

I thank you once again, Mr Braithwaite – he said the next day, at sundown – for your hospitality, your most earnest hard work on behalf of my small household. The squire, also, most naturally, is to be thanked, as well as the estimable Mr Smith; but principally you, and *your* household, supporting as I assume it must your noble efforts in this new line of work. I assume both parents and siblings remain in good health, and happiness? Certainly your mention of them in our brief correspondence leads me to hope so. Always I seek to discover a home amongst those of good cheer, and this estimable community appears to meet my longstanding criterion most admirably.

Yet, sir, I appear to be getting far ahead of myself; my sincerest apologies. Please – be seated. You will notice I have added the requisite small appurtenances to the stout and serviceable furniture provided by the squire. Antimacassars, arm-guards, ashtrays and the like. I hope they will blend in, as I myself hope to do.

But listen, as I prattle on like a maid loath to be about her work!

I am Porlock – Magnus Porlock, Mr Braithwaite, of ancient family and perhaps a dozen countries on what you here in England so quaintly like to call the continent. Latterly of London, of course, in which bustling metropolis I met through his city cousin, at his club, your esteemed squire, and thus made a very useful acquaintance.

Now, of course – and for the foreseeable future – I hail from Yorkshire, and the fine settlement of Westerdale more particularly. It is a small community, but I hope hospitable – even friendly – to the outsider, and thus far your work has been of immense value in speeding along my introductions.

Yesterday evening I made the acquaintance of the landlord at the inn, and beside its roaring fire, that of an estate factor (there to discuss some significant business, judging by the line of ale-pots standing before him) as well as three or four stout yeoman farmers who seem to typify the Yorkshiremen of this area.

I remain, therefore, eminently grateful to you, Mr Braithwaite, for affecting my entrance into society. And for seeing to my comforts and needs, such as they are, within the walls of this charming cottage, located perfectly beneath the beetling brow of Sugarloaf Hill. Had I lifted a small building in the air with my own two hands, only to place it down upon a map in the place suited perfectly to my every need, I could have done no better.

Bravo, sir – bravo!

Now, do you wish to avail yourself of refreshment? I would inform you of my purpose here, or at least some of my purposes, in order that this small and welcoming community will talk naturally not of fairy-wild speculations, but fact, the sure bedrock of belonging.

Please – eat, drink, I beg of you.

When you are comfortable, I shall begin.

12

To look at me, you might suppose – what? You will see a being of a certain height, assuredly; some import – I should hope so. I have worked long and hard in this world to make a mark on its surface. But what of the rest? You may say, a foreigner. I would retort – absolutely so. But also a speaker of your fine tongue – no Dickens, or Miss Brontë, perhaps – and a lover of its tales and verses for many a year, nevertheless. Deportment? Fitting a man of my height, slim in the body, saturnine in the face. Wiry, even? I grant you it is so!

But beyond the face I present to the world, what comprises this vessel called Porlock?

I began six decades ago, slightly more – in a nearby country. My father, and his before him, one link in a great and unbreakable chain reaching into the mists of mountainous lands, steeped in history and in legend. Alas, as the last century drew on, that land suffered in dignity as yours waxed fat and powerful upon the stage. Fortunes rose, and fell; castles, once rampant, high and jagged against faces of stone that tore apart the skies, now crumbled and toppled into the breach; families locked fast in the arms of plenty, withered in empty rooms.

I, the last – certainly feeling so – of my starving race ransacked each library, each nook and cranny of print, for news of the future. There I found, in abundance, words and pictures of your English books – ah, newspapers and periodicals! the triple-decker novel, the penny dreadful! – that took me, after I had drunk deep of them (yet still not slaked my thirst) across the vast continent to London.

You are young, my friend, and perhaps not so schooled in the ways of your vast, teeming metropolis.

I, too, was taken aback at its grandeur, its squalor, and all the bustling runs of rats and dogs and slops and hay, of mire and gold and snuff exploding in the nose, of all bounty laid before me – too much! Too much.

I slowed, obtaining a room of sorts – its cold, windowless space suited the needs of my mind – and settled down to study from life what before had penetrated my mind only through the printed word.

I found myself in the hamlet known as Streatham. I could not pronounce its name, at first, but was soon set right when I ventured from my dank lair into the better-lit high road, and encountered a jovial man beneath a gas-lamp, balancing a thin wooden tray upon his knee. Covering its surface was an array of implements for smoking: matches, short and stubby clay pipes, almost too small for a man to pack with tobacco, twists of stiff cleaning wool for twining through the apertures. He looked up at me, appearing at first to shrink back a little into himself.

'Do not be afraid, sir. Please. I wish merely to know the name of this district.'

I must have sounded, to his ears, like some nightmare book-cover come to life and vomiting forth its contents without cease. He told me, then retreated to his shell. When he realised I did not wish to smoke – what use such stimulants, to one such as I? – he became first angry, then resigned, then in the way of many, curious.

'Whatchew doin ere, then?' he asked. I noticed his hand begin to fold the lid of the tray over his objects in a most ingenious fashion, fingers seemingly working of their own accord, and then his other hand steal towards a pocket. I did not wait for it to clasp whatever blade might lie within, but seized his wrist.

'I thank you, friend, for this information. I will look for you when I return, and am more familiar with the district.'

I released him, and the man grabbed his wares and ran for the mouth of a dark alley. I could have pursued him, but to what end? He had given me the key, and the next day I left my damp cave at sunset for the nearest library, looked out records of the place, its doings and concerns, prominent citizens as well as those of a less reputable nature, who nonetheless might aid me in the process of becoming – acclimatised, shall we say.

For this London, it seemed, was a stew of opportunity beyond any my countrymen could imagine. I stayed for a while in the cellar, then when I had learned from others of my kind where better lodging, and food, was to be had, I moved to a lofty garret in a row of town houses high above the common. From its window I could see those opportunities twinkling and drawing me onwards, as insects to the burning wick (never mind its hot globe, or blackened wings). My landlady was an old, half-blind and trusting woman, with much invested, too dry to present any challenge and too slight to venture up to the empty attic beyond one single time in a month.

And what, now settled, was I doing?

Everything!

I had the language at my command – I require but little sleep, and can sate myself on a single meal once a month – so sat and burrowed through print like never before. Amazing, young man, how on the acquisition of a new skill, all else in life seems bent on feeding its improvement! I would imagine your own shoes, similarly, now clean of the detritus of the farmyard, spoke to you of advancement, and new knowledge; how your suit – far above the common labourer's bumpkin attire – whispered in each moment of the promise of a better life?

I was not discerning, but devoured everything – as keen to spirit back up the stair a grubby broadsheet, printed by monkeys on crude stock, and parroting the most bigoted of political opinions, as I was to procure the master's third instalment of some panoramic story, the mistress's lambent verse, even the minister's sermons burnt upon the page. My brain was afire with words! I became, I suppose, besides a connoisseur of print itself, a sort of dealer in it. I found the stock of the circulating libraries, after a good many lendings and consumption by various hands, stained with tobacco, soot-smutches – even blood – still quite recoverable, though the libraries begged me to take the ragged books off their hands. I learned a little of paper-treatment, bookbinding, and a great deal of the art of haggling as I restored these works to new life, after their brief interruption.

Neither was I shy of branching out. I noticed, on occasion, a fine lithographic plate – perhaps a woodland scene, or the spires of some great cathedral rendered by a painstaking hand – remaining untouched at the heart of an otherwise worthless book. It was the work of a moment to scoop it from its grave, and restore it to a new and better life in a fine frame on a merchant's wall, or tacked between a pair of windows in a coffee shop; or, indeed, living again anywhere at all. Gradually my stock of such treasures rose, and began to displace in my business the erstwhile fundamental of words themselves.

It was on one such occasion I noticed this trend, and on identifying it, lost everything in a single, terrible gamble whose reverberations ultimately brought me here. Listen, if you will, a little further, for what lessons I have learned I am willing to pour into your ear.

You have realised that I am not as other men are. Not as you, yourself, so plainly must be: rising to work – though I work! – and taking a crust or two for sustenance – though I, too, must eat! – and coming home to family and hearth at day's end, tired but content. This is a life to which I as a foreigner in so many ways was never born.

But it has its compensations.

The new direction of my business took me to the heart of the city on occasions. I had discovered amongst the good people of London a new, and seemingly insatiable, taste for the things of the orient. I saw in the coffee shops and those parlours to which I was occasionally invited, cups and plates decorated with blue-and-white pagodas, quaint higgledy bridges and all manner of flowering delights. On fans, fireguards, even internal doors – lacquer and dragons in profusion! It was a positive mania, Mr Braithwaite. I knew a little of the decorative arts in Japan from an acquaintance, a Mr Peacock, who years before had served in an Anglican mission to Japan and himself become fascinated with the style of art known as 'floating world'. In these magisterial pictures, carved, inked and printed by the thousand, we find the demi-monde of an earlier Japan: courtesans and wrestlers, tea-houses, docks and toppling waves and low fights in darkened alleys. In short, all the world's nasty, lucrative pastimes, shaped to art with the highest skill, and more saleable than anything I had yet encountered.

A client mentioned in passing that a certain shop in Westminster – by Great Smith Street, I recall – held inside its walls a secret which, he suspected, might interest me greatly.

'Why?'

I did not feel the need to sugarcoat my true self in his presence. Though he was not of my kind, he had swum through enough sewers to know the hard realities of this life.

'Why?'

He threw back the last of his rum. Mine, as ever, remained untouched. 'Because you've been fooling around with second-hand sources, my friend, that's why. This is *the* source.'

'Whatever do you mean?' I leant forward, pressing him with the force of my gaze.

'I mean why trifle with bodgers and deadbeats and second-rate dealers, down on their luck? This is gold. She's gold, though to be fair to you, I haven't clapped eyes on the woman myself.'

'It is a woman?'

'Oh, aye. And from the land o'the rising sun itself.'

It was not yet late, and I left him there immediately, without another word. I arrived in the vicinity by trap, but needed no such contrivance to cover distances when my blood was up. In no time, I skirted the abbey and the Mother of Parliaments, and was scouting the darker backstreets for the dealer's lair. The road was straight, then grew crooked, but in a ginnel on the second bend I found it: a doorway, partially obscured by straw-filled crates, with a low black candle-lamp glowing steadily. Perhaps my rummy acquaintance could be trusted, after all.

I looked about, once, twice, then realised in this section of town – despite the grandeur not five hundred yards away – there were no eyes on anything in the alley; it was not meant to be seen. There was a fat grille set at head height, an iron turn-handle below. I twisted it open and stepped inside, expecting damp stone and cobwebs, perhaps hanging beams or a fractured skylight or two, letting in the miserable smoky night. Instead it was bright and inviting. Someone had set new lanterns, trimmed and even, in sconces down the corridor, which itself was paved with immaculate white stone. It was smooth not dusty underfoot, and no footsteps had left their mark. At the far end was a smaller door, of a woman's size, and I ducked through this aperture without bothering to knock. It led to a spacious chamber dominated by a fire banked high with spitting logs.

In front of the fire, with her back to the door – and thus faceless – was a woman. She spoke as I entered, and her voice was high, mellifluous, like a windchime stirred by a knowing hand, but cut underneath with the sharpness of river branches forcing their way through jagged ice.

'You have taken your time,' she said. I did not know how to respond – how could I? – but she laughed anyway, standing up beside her chair and laying one long arm on the mantelpiece, finally turning to face me.

I knew immediately she was one of my kind; moreover, one so far above (or below) me in force of habit, of practice, if you will, that I could not match her lightning speed, the weightless efficiency of her murder. Yet she smiled, showing sharp white teeth; held out that same elegant arm, its skin of a slightly darker, golden hue than my own wind-beaten covering; brushed long black hair from her shoulder; stepped up before me.

'You appear surprised,' she said, and I saw laughter dance behind her teeth in the black maw of what she was. 'I mean no harm to you, but you must realise there are not so many of us we can afford to ignore the presence of another, within our home city. Your ratlike friend, I assume, tipped you to my presence – ?'

I nodded. The blood, stirred at first in my shocked veins, now coursed freely. I sensed wind and danger and allure, all whipped together like some mysterious frothing liquid. She turned again, took a decanter of black fluid from a table, poured me a glass. I was too numb to resist.

'Sit,' she said. 'Drink. We have much to discuss.'

I sat, the black liquid drowning my senses in warmth.

'Do we?'

But it was a conclusion I never reached. My life, it seemed, was at a crossroads. I was no longer the starving immigrant; not the greenhorn in the city, whimpering and slithering from hovel to hovel; nor, indeed, the fledgeling man of business, scratching a living from crumbs that fell from other's tables. But in my bones I knew this was a development of moment. There was weight, promise, in the woman's stare. I looked across the fire at her and blanched. Behind the slim, deceptive oval of her face burned a fire far stronger than the one in the grate.

'You know that we do. I am Matsu, a common enough name for a woman from my country. It is not the name of my birth, but neither is Porlock yours.'

'How – ?'

She gestured, and the coals gave forth a hiss.

'Names have no meaning for our kind. I have tracked every one who has come through this city, and the few who remain from before. It is important we keep our heads low, take the minimum of food, lest we alert the others to our presence. It is important, too, that more than bodies trade and flow across the boundaries of nations. Look around you. I could ordinarily move from London to my homeland perhaps once every few years – each year, at most – on my own terms, openly, without arousing suspicion. But in the service of trade, my options are limitless, my opportunities manifold. Come.'

She rose, and was across the room in a moment, pulling aside a great hessian curtain to reveal a row of high tea chests marked with Japanese figures. She flipped up the rim of the first, pulled several boxed prints (heavy with wood and lacquer) from the rustling depths of the crate as though disturbing a fly with a handkerchief. I walked over to look. They were astounding – both huge and tiny, bold and infinitely subtle in colour and line. The first showed a courtesan posing beneath a cherry tree (it seemed to be evening), one lean arm holding a parasol against the blossom, the other lifting aside the top of her robe to reveal the swell of a breast. The second showed two wrestlers locked in combat, the hard glossy lines of their hair rounded and sharp as the contours of their bodies. What I assumed was a second stood behind, a perplexed look on his face.

'Of these, I have hundreds.'

She was casual, almost dismissive, as though such fabulous merchandise was somehow common in the world. Perhaps in her world, and the world which could be mine, it was indeed so. She walked down the row, pulled back another bunch of hessian, and revealed a different, smaller crate. This one was constructed from polished black wood, with a gold handle set into its top.

'Of this kind, not so many.'

She lifted the lid with reverence, taking a single print between both palms and carrying it to a map-table lit by its own dedicated gas-lamp. In the warm yellow light, the print was shocking. A creature of the night, clad in black robes, trailing cobweb and dirty earth behind him, was crawling down the wall of a mausoleum under a bloody moon. The sky was ripped apart by ragged clouds, and at the foot of the wall – terrified, hands frozen beneath her screaming face – lay a woman awaiting her dreadful fate. The lines were the cleanest, most artful I had ever seen applied by human hand, and yet depicted a scene no sane man would ever wish to see, let alone pay to obtain, to cherish in some magnificent cherrywood frame, and hang upon the parlour wall.

Matsu looked at me and smiled.

It was then that I knew I was lost.

12

I have heard tales, in passing, from those who live as I do – of hypnotism, mesmerism, complete control through some otherworldly, unknowable mechanism. I have seen the man who claims to make metal yield with his mind perform circus tricks on the screen, grown men and women clucking around a stage like farmyard animals, or grunting like swine. I laughed along at the time, dismissing such tricks as mere stagecraft, beneath someone of my age, and my experience.

No longer. When I think of it, my mind contracts around this bloodied scene like a fist, attempting in vain to stop a handful of water from flowing away. There is pain aplenty. And it, too, will flow as it must. It is flowing now.

In no time at all, Matsu had me in her power.

I struggle to think what happened, how it took place. My memory, stout as an oaken door to which I alone possess the key, quivers with the weakness of a sapling when I think of it. The art-print of our kind, its colours blood-rich, beguiling; the flickering of the lamp on the pale table; a sense of speed, and motion, faint impressions of stones set close together rushing by like clouds; then simply nothing.

'Porlock,' she said.

I must have remained inert, unresponsive in my unknown state. For she tried my other supposed name. 'Magnus.' The sibilance, fructified with all the chill compulsion of her cutting voice, brought me back from the gloom.

'What! What – where is this place?'

There was no light, but we needed none. She had transported me to some cave, a rock hole blasted from the mountains far from the city; in another country altogether, for all I knew. The mouth of it cut a black hole out of the fading sky. The floor underneath me was beaten dirt, and some care had evidently been taken to stack each object around me back from the entrance, so it could not be seen: packing crates; valises; trunks of every kind. A broken lamp sat here, its glass starred, staring; a fine cloak there, rent in a dozen places. It smelled of despair, earth, animal vitality. I sensed, for all its squalor, that it was her true home.

'We have business,' she said, beckoning. I rose and followed. The cave-mouth disappeared behind us. We flitted down a thready mountain path, until we reached a road, of sorts. I had no notion of what was to come, though my waking brain computed the odd location of the cave, the stacks of abandoned goods, and attempted to put numbers together into a proper sum. It was not correct. She shoved me bodily between two stout pines, forced my head down below the level of the roughly-macadamed surface. It was full dark, but far in the distance I was able to make out a moving shape, black still against the wider black of night, but crunching through it, small diamonds of grey and yellowish fire darting between the spaces of the trees.

'Quiet, until they are upon us,' Matsu said, her small hand iron on my shoulder. The coach rolled and thundered, ever nearer, till it was suddenly upon us in a blaze of jolting lanterns and whinnying horses, the coachman lashing round the bend.

'Now!'

We sprang in unison, and the world burst apart. Coachman screaming, whip lost to the commotion; horses breaking the traces, their necks corded, teeth thick-speckled with foam; luggage rising like a stack of stones blown from the riverbed, and dashed over the rapids – box after box spinning high in every direction, striking tree-trunks, wheels, dashing open on the gritty tar of the road. She turned my head within this chaos to the door which lay uppermost on the coach, and from which the passengers spilled, half a dozen tumbling souls, shrieking, arms pinwheeling for purchase, necks laid open to attack.

I will not describe it; will not even recall such a scene, beyond an arc of blood and fear, the terrible ripping sounds of the people's demise.

I next came to inside the cave. Matsu was throwing around pieces of leather and cordage, tearing away labels and any sign of identification from the luggage. When she finished, the gross wreckage of the cave was merely rearranged, so as to hinder discovery. As to the broken lives, bodies doubtless drained and buried beneath some lonely pine, she gave not the slightest attention.

'Gather yourself, for we return to London.'

I would have been better lying down to die on the filthy earth of the cave floor, or my dim – and dear! – first, pathetic hovel; even some bleak anonymous street, as I would returning to that gilded hell. But there we returned, and my life as a slave to her base passions began.

The days were tolerable. Surrounded by art, and the soft crackle of logs, the papery bloom of the tea chest, as well as a certain orderly, business-like approach to the hoarding and release of treasures, I could delude myself. If only it had been perpetual day!

But by night, when the businesswoman in Matsu fled, and the beast emerged – then would I have done away with myself, to rid my mind of her malign influence. I believe she thrived in the darkness all the more with a companion, however unwilling. We returned, now and again, to the cave, but more often haunted lonely spots within the city itself: beneath the great bridges, where cast-off souls huddled around tiny fires; empty wharves, waiting like insects for the sun to warm and enliven them, stippled here and there with the corpses of nightwatchmen, or stevedores; in byways, alleys, the mouths of conveniences, under warehouse eaves, the meanest – but most fruitful – of slatternly ginnels.

Oh! that I had not seen these things, done them, with a light yet implacable touch at my back.

I have no sense of time in this period – it may have been days, or perhaps not days, but months, certainly; a grim procession of such periods compressed tightly against one another, like the pleats of some infernal accordion, and I the shrieking tune it vomited forth upon the world. We danced, ripped, drank our way through the entrails of the century.

When exactly I came back to myself, I do not know. It was in the wake of hundreds of lives lost, that much I know. I recall, like the stuttering frames of the new cinematograph – though blessedly free of the ticklings of a pianist – the moment, had I but known it, of my release.

'Stop – stop, I beg you! Please!'

She was crouched, quivering, in the mouth of the evening's second alley, a yawning shape that gave on a stretch of cobbles strewn with broken wheels. Matsu looked up from her crouch, deadly white metallic hatred in her eyes.

'What? Have you no energy for the hunt? I can remedy that!'

'No.'

It was a single word, but in its utterance was the ring of new steel. I said it again, and as defiance rose, an unstoppable phoenix from the ashes of my ruined soul, so the rage built like air-blown embers in her eyes. She stood; they shone, deadly lamps brighter, yet colder, than the hardened streets around us. I did not care. Something else shone out from my soul – defiance, certainly; I had borne enough of her deadly game. But perhaps hope, also – a scent, just the tiniest, delicate note, of some future unburdened by the demon to whom I had been unwillingly shackled.

Finding I know not what strength, I prised her hand from the hasp of another sickening charnel-house door. The inhabitants never knew how close they sailed to death that evening. Walking the rim of Hell, as some poet of Matsu's land had it. But I pushed in hard at her wiry flesh. It took all my strength, but some force inside me propelled me onwards. We tumbled into the darkness and stench, till I could no longer see her face, even the outline of the supple, beautiful limbs with which she had chained me to my fate.

Finally, by some vast metal grating that straddled the alley, we stopped.

'What? Haven't you the stomach to feed tonight? No matter! There is always tomorrow.'

She laughed, high and hard and brittle. I flinched. It was as though I heard this devil's caterwaul for the first time.

'No. I say no – tonight, tomorrow, forever. No more. I will follow you no longer.'

There was silence for a moment. Water dripped from an overfilled rain-butt to the floor; something skittered between my feet. Then she exploded like the gates of that selfsame Hell bursting under the weight of the world's sin. I have no words for the force of her – nor, seemingly, did she. I am still amazed no-one charged the alleyway, thinking the occupants of London zoo had been let loose upon the city. She ripped, tore, bellowed; she lashed at my face, my chest and arms with steely, locked fingers, battered me about the torso with the force of innumerable blows, all the while screaming in a terrible banshee wail that rang in my ears like hammer-blows upon a rail. I stood my ground, taking all that she had to give; pushing back, but not attacking in my turn, except when she lunged for my throat, teeth flashing in the flickering light. Then I, myself, was loosed, bore down upon her own neck with an instinctive snap.

For a moment there was nothing.

Then I heard distinctly the crunch of a trap starting up in some impossibly far-distant street, the whinny of a horse. I was doused with a torrent of boiling, acid blood – a veritable fountain, jetting in a stream from a wide gap at the base of her throat. I seized the opportunity and forced her to her knees, to the ground, intent only on stopping this madness. But as I pressed her body down it began to jerk and then to twitch, the gush of lifeblood – still hitting me in freshets – now pumping, now dribbling away to a trickle. I stood, mute, astonished. She lay at my feet, the cataract spent, dammed at some unimaginable point in the heavens.

I did not linger, looking as I must as though I had worked a full day in the slaughterhouse, yet was completely prepared for a further shift. At the alley's mouth I paused only for a moment to gather what little sense came to me.

'I am sorry to have stopped your life,' I said – was it out loud, or only in my mind? – 'but I do not wish to interrupt that of anyone else.'

It seemed a feeble enough conclusion, though I knew it to be true. I stripped off my overcoat, wiping away as much of the bonehouse filth as I could, and cast it behind a mound of refuse, ran my face through the rain-barrel, then set off at a run to the farthest side of the city.

I have ceased running, at last.

I have come to a place where life walks in a more measured fashion, and is regarded as more than a swift meal, a passing lightning-bolt of pleasure. I have come to a stop, and perhaps to begin something better. I have come to this blessed dale, Mr Braithwaite, in order to disappear.

13

The room was black; no fire had been laid, and whatever light the lamp might have given, had it been lit, was absent. I sat in the blackness with my mind reeling. I'd helped remake the little cottage, yes, but what did that cottage have to do with the vast, sprawling and utterly mad world of the tale just told?

Nothing, lass! Nothing. I'd been transported, whisked away like a bairn on the wings of a fairy tale, wide-eyed, with my hand up to my mouth, disbelieving. But that isn't right. I did believe. I knew, lined by the tiniest spark of some residual light, that across the room from my chair was a man – more than a man, perhaps less – the like of which we hope never escapes from our nightmares.

And yet.

I could hear him breathe. I knew, as he knew, as well, that now his tale was told, there were only two routes out of that room: friendship, or a quick and hopefully merciful death, my remains buried somewhere in the shadow of Sugarloaf Hill.

Eventually, he spoke.

'I, too, hear your breathing, Mr Braithwaite.'

'Please, sir – call me Edward.'

I sensed the air crinkle about his mouth.

'Edward, then. So now you know my story. My nature.'

'Yes, sir.'

'You also must know, then, that I mean you no harm, nor to any of your kin, nor the good people of this dale.'

'I know that, sir.'

And I did. Hadn't he taken every trouble, in his letters, with the squire, Mr Smith, with me and the silent, tender bosom of the village as he passed through after the setting sun? What could he gain from disturbing that now?

I stood, and taking the tinderbox from my pocket, lit one or two candles about the room. As his face emerged from the darkness, I could see lines of worry set in its olive skin, the age resting behind, like an artist's first, more truthful strokes under the top layers. But it seemed kind. I wondered how long he had really looked for this sanctuary.

'You must go, now,' Mr Porlock said. 'I have taken you from your family for too long.'

I bowed and quickly put on my cap, worked my arms into my coat.

'Will that be all, then, sir?' I asked. I think I knew the answer, lass, before I even asked the question.

'I may require your services, now and then, if that is agreeable.'

It wasn't a question, and as I nodded and took my leave, there thrilled through me some shiver of secret knowledge. I'd see him again, I knew.

I would see him again.

14

The sandwiches were long gone. Not even a smear of pease-pudding remained on Jean's neatly-folded greaseproof paper. But there was a bit of coffee in the flask, and Edward didn't object when I unscrewed the top and offered him the last of it. It was still bright out, though the sun had reached far enough into the sky for the brow of Sugarloaf to start eating into its path. If we sat for another hour it would disappear, and I wasn't sure I wanted to stay beyond sunset, that inevitable slide into gloom, with the rough track and the cottage not half a mile distant.

'Thanks, love,' Edward said when he'd finished his coffee. It must have been lukewarm, but still. He held the Thermos cap in both hands, thumbs hooked over the top, and smiled. 'Hope I didn't bore you silly.'

'What!'

I hadn't heard a tale this good since John Major assured us the economy was in good hands, and we were heading for a classless society. I said so. Edward laughed.

'Are we setting off back, then?'

I nodded.

'Just a sec.'

I screwed the lid back on, folded up the paper and napkins into the cotton bag. She'd want it back, I knew. I popped the sun-visor into the Micra's roof. It hit the mouse-fur lining with a soft *whump*, and I shivered a little, despite the warmth of the departing sun. I started the engine, let it warm up a bit before putting the car in gear.

'Same way back?'

He nodded, but didn't say anything. His talk was done for the day, it looked like. I got us turned around in the mouth of the roadway and headed back through Westerdale, turned right at the junction and made our way across the valley floor towards Castleton. He didn't remark on Ellerstang as we passed, or the war memorial, the stonemason's, and five minutes later we'd parked beside the alley, and I was helping him inside.

Aunty Jean bustled out and took over. I heard them talking in the kitchen, took a seat in Edward's high-backed chair beside the fire. Someone had built up a nice bank of coals. I leant back and closed my eyes for a good long think. I wasn't sure what to make of Edward's tale. It was thrilling, certainly; I'd never forget it – not the danger or the sadness, the violence, the soaring emotions. But I wondered if he'd been inspired by my lecturers, the mention of the literature of his youth, maybe a need to show a couple of softy southerners a real Yorkshire story.

They came back in a minute later, so I had to stop my maundering, and shift.

'Tea in a bit, Jean says. You staying?'

'Yeah. My essay can wait till tomorrow.'

'Alright, then.'

He reached for his glasses case and popped it open, placing a strange octagonal pair of spectacles on the bridge of his nose. With his twin flares of gingery-white hair, the glasses accentuating his nose, he looked like an odd bird that had flitted in for a quick look around the room. He took up the topmost letter from the pile on his side-table. Something occurred to me.

'In your – ah, story, Edward?'

'Oh, aye?'

'Porlock, your gentleman. How old was he?'

'Oh, about sixty, I should say. Quite well-preserved, he was, mind.'

'And that's how old he looked before he got here. From London – right?'

'That's it.'

'And this was right after the First World War, in 1920?'

'Summat bothering you, lass?'

'Oh, nothing – not really. It's just, well. He seemed like a young man in the story. Sort of vital, not old, you know? I'm not sure someone would be that way, if they'd had that hard sort of a life.'

He took off his glasses and gestured at the letter with one leg, then spoke rather thoughtfully.

'He never really seems his age, you know. Looks well, speaks well. Writes well too. Like a younger man, and a gentleman, I'd say.' Edward passed the letter over to me. It was beautiful: carefully written on thick, expensive paper, a lovely creamy bone-white, but not brittle or old. The ink seemed fresh, almost glittery in the firelight.

It was dated two days before.

About the Author

JAMES RODERICK BURNS is the author of one flash fiction collection, *To Say Nothing of the Dog,* and five collections of short-form poetry, most recently, *Crows at Dusk*. He graduated with Distinction from the Oxford MSt in Creative Writing. His stories have twice been nominated for the Pushcart Prize, and he currently serves as Staff Reader in Poetry for *Ploughshares*. He lives in Edinburgh with his wife and daughter.

He can be found on Twitter @JamesRoderickB.

www.ingramcontent.com/pod-product-compliance
Lightning Source LLC
LaVergne TN
LVHW091048150826
845673LV00002B/499

* 9 7 8 8 1 1 9 6 5 4 2 6 0 *